JUNE DAVIES

THE WARMSLEYS OF PEDLARS DOWN

Complete and Unabridged

LINFORD
Leicester

First published in Great Britain in 2017

First Linford Edition
published 2018

A catalogue record for this book is available
from the British Library.

ISBN 978–1–4448–3543–4

Published by
F. A. Thorpe (Publishing)
Anstey, Leicestershire

Set by Words & Graphics Ltd.
Anstey, Leicestershire
Printed and bound in Great Britain by
T. J. International Ltd., Padstow, Cornwall

This book is printed on acid-free paper

1

Spring sunshine was warming the uneven roofs and crooked chimneys of Pedlars Down, spilling upon the manor house's brown and white timbers and leaded windows, coaxing forth swaths of daffodils in Rachel's flower garden and shining upon the billowing laundry Gladdie was pinning out on the drying-frame. The instant the gawky maid finished pegging the last nightshirt, stooped to take up the empty willow wash-baskets and scurried indoors, a round freckled face popped up from beyond the holly bushes.

'She's gone, Lenny — but stay down till I make sure nobody else is about!' he hissed, emerging from the bushes with a roly-poly brown pup at his side and sauntering out into the open. Jonas Warmsley was a sturdy lad for his thirteen years. Narrowing his eyes against the strong early sunlight, he surveyed the small timber-framed house with its cluster of stables and barns, and beyond them the gardens, meadows, pasture and woodlands. Not a soul in sight. However, Jonas's sharp ears caught the sound of voices a distance away. Probably Pa, brother Edward and the journeyman working in the apple orchards.

'It's all clear, Lenny! Hurry up,' he went on, glancing back to a gnarled oak. 'We dash straight across to that big door, see? Well?' he added, a tad vexed when his new pal didn't make a move. 'Are you coming or not?'

'I'm not sure about going in now, Jonas. You won't get into trouble if you're caught, but *I* will!' Much smaller, and the younger of the pair by a couple of years, Lenny edged cautiously from behind the oak's mighty trunk. 'Grandmother Burford told us we were never to set foot anywhere near Pedlars Down. She told us that as soon as Felix and I came to

Withencroft with Madge and Malcolm after the wedding. 'We Burfords from Withencroft don't have anything to do with the family at Pedlars Down,' she said. 'Mind you remember, and keep well away from the Warmsleys!''

'Oh, that's only because of the feud,' dismissed Jonas, absently tossing a twig for Rupert, who was whining and wagging at his side. 'The two families haven't spoken to each other for ages. But why has the old granny forbidden *you* to come here? *You're* not a Burford!'

'I am now, and so is Felix!' insisted Lenny, hitching up shabby, too-large breeches. 'Ever since our sister wed Malcolm Burford. 'Sides, we live at Withencroft now, so we have to do as Grandmother says — she's fierce, Jonas!'

'Aye, she is a bit,' he conceded, but was not to be thwarted. 'She's never going to find out, though, is she? Nobody is. And you do want to see the gold coin, don't you?'

'Is it really pirates' treasure?' Lenny wavered, gazing over to the five-sided bay window at the west gable of the old manor house. 'And it's just inside there? Inside that queer window?'

'Wedged up in the beam where Christopher Warmsley left it hundreds of years ago,' he replied in a low voice, adding darkly, 'on the very night the ghastly feud between the Warmsleys and the Burfords said!'

'What'll your mam and dad do if they find me?'

'My ma passed away when I was a bairn, Pa's working in the orchard with Edward, and it's market day so my sister Rachel's gone out!' With that, Jonas turned and, gripping Lenny's wrist, hauled his friend out across the coarse grass towards the manor house, weaving between grazing sheep who scarce batted an eyelid.

The heavy iron-bound oaken door closed behind them with a thud that echoed around the stone-flagged great hall. After the warm, brilliant sunshine, the cavernous oblong room with its massive fireplace, gigantic Jacobean long-table, huge settles, chests and cupboards was cold and dark. Away down at the furthest end, sunlight was flooding through the stained-glass panes of the five-sided compass window and splashing vivid pools of blues, reds, greens and gold across the worn-smooth stone flags.

Jonas's boots rang out as he marched the length of the great hall, with Lenny following warily in his wake. The pals wore well-patched hand-me-down shirts and breeches and were clad exactly alike, save for the battered broad-brimmed hat clamped down over Lenny's mop of curly chestnut hair.

Scurrying past the Jacobean long-table, Lenny asked, 'Why have you got buckets on the table?'

'It rained last night,' answered Jonas without a backward glance. 'The roof leaks.'

'Why don't you mend it?'

'Same reason nowt else gets mended.

Can't afford it.' He shrugged, stopping in his tracks at the alcove created by the compass window and pointing to an oak upright at the edge of the deep five-sided bay. 'There it is, right high up. Pirate's gold!'

A heavy gold coin was firmly wedged into the grain of the oak beam. It was gleaming and glinting and glowing in the sunlight pouring through all five panels of old glass, and Lenny's eyes widened like the organ-stops in the village church.

'Why is it up there?'

'Because Christopher Warmsley put it there, of course!' replied Jonas impatiently, adding vaguely, 'The Warmsleys and the Burfords were cousins, friendly in them days. But then they started fighting. There were debts and wagers and duels and all sorts. Rupert! Give that here!' He bent to extract a hank of soggy wool from his pup's mouth and shoved it back into Rachel's mending basket, right at the bottom underneath the holey stockings and shirts.

'I've never seen owt like them!' exclaimed Lenny, pointing to queer-looking chairs set around a spinning wheel within the compass window. 'Whyever have they only got three legs?'

'Sit down!' Jonas grinned, shoving aside Rachel's mending basket and dropping heavily onto one of the turned plum-wood chairs. 'See? With only three legs, they don't rock about on the uneven flags.'

'That's clever, isn't it?' said Lenny. 'This must be a grand spot for drawin', it's so light with all these windows. Ay up, isn't this your sister coming with the lady from church?'

'Can't be.' Jonas shot to his feet and peered through one of the clear panes in dismay. Sure enough, Rachel and Agnes Whitehead, the churchwarden's daughter, were strolling up the beech walk laden with an assortment of baskets and parcels. 'She's never back this early on market day!'

'What'll we do, Jonas?' panicked

Lenny, accidentally kicking over Rachel's sewing basket and heap of mending, stooping to hastily pile it all back higgledy-piggledy. 'She'll catch us for sure! I'll get into terrible trouble at Withencroft. And what'll your sister do when she finds me here?'

'Rachel won't know who you are,' answered Jonas confidently, glancing down at his companion. 'She won't realise you're a Burford. Besides, she's not *going* to find us!' Gripping Lenny's wrist, he sprinted back the length of the hall and around the screen into a shadowy cross-passage with doors, nooks and corners leading from it.

'Where are we going?' wailed Lenny as they plunged around a press into near blackness, with Rupert gambolling and barking excitedly about their legs.

'Secret passage. Just follow Rupert, he knows the way!' instructed Jonas, revelling in such unexpected adventures. 'Pa says this was a priest's hole in the olden days and a hidey-hole for spies during the Civil War! It comes out beyond the stables. Don't worry, Lenny. Nobody'll ever know you've been here,' he added kindly as they pelted down a flight of rough escape steps. 'Even if Rachel did find out, I don't reckon she'd fret us much. My sister nags and mithers summat chronic, but she's not a bad old stick really.'

* * *

'Marjorey's certainly a comely girl, from what I saw of her when the Burfords came into church last Sunday,' Rachel was saying as she and Agnes Whitehead strolled beneath the beeches up towards the homely little manor house.

'She has a fine jaunty walk too! There's a maid who'll keep Malcolm on his toes and not be a whit put out by Grandmother Burford's sharp tongue,' went on Rachel sagely. 'Although I only caught a glimpse of Marjorey — I didn't like staring.'

'Why not? The rest of the congregation was,' chuckled Agnes, brushing away a wisp of fair hair straying from beneath her fashionable bonnet. 'It's not every day one of the Burford boys brings home a bride from across the water.'

'Is that where Marjorey's from? New Brighton?' enquired Rachel, shifting the weight of the heavy basket on her arm. 'I haven't heard a thing about her.'

'Oh, it's terribly sad. Reverend Greenhalgh was telling Mother and Father about Marjorey's family when he came to supper. Apparently her father was captain on the packet to Ireland,' explained Agnes. 'He and his wife drowned when the boat went down during those terrible storms several years ago. Marjorey was little more than a child herself then, but as the eldest it fell upon her to raise the younger ones. There were no other relatives.'

'Losing both parents!' murmured Rachel sympathetically. 'When Ma passed away, the boys and I still had Pa and each other.' A faint smile twitched her lips as she recalled those hectic, rumbustious years of cooking, washing, mending, nursing and bringing up her two younger brothers. 'Even as a child, Edward always had his nose in some book or other and never was an iota of bother. But Jonas . . . He was still an infant when we lost Ma, but from the day he started toddling, he got up to mischief! Even now,' she went on, shaking her head in exasperation. 'I still can't take my eyes off him for what he slopes away with the village lads when he should be doing chores.'

'Jonas is just a boy,' reproved Agnes mildly as she and Rachel approached the manor house. 'He has a good heart.'

'Hmm, that's as may be, but it doesn't get his chores done,' said Rachel, climbing the steps to the low oaken door but breaking off when she spotted two figures and a pup dawdling away across the clover pasture. 'That's Jonas — he should be helping Pa and Edward! And who's that little lad with him?'

'I can't recognise him from this distance,' remarked Agnes, peering through her small silver-rimmed spectacles. 'Perhaps he's the new Burford boy, Felix — Marjorey's young brother?'

'Jonas knows better than to bring a Burford onto Pedlars Down,' responded Rachel grimly. 'You know how Pa feels about them. Jonas!' she hailed her brother sharply, halting the startled youngsters in their tracks. 'Never mind skylarking. Get yourself off to the orchard and help Pa!'

'I'm going!' shouted Jonas, grabbing Lenny's arm and haring off in the direction of the apple orchard.

'That lad'll be the death of me,' muttered Rachel as the two women entered the manor house and started along the cross-passage to the kitchen, which like the rest of the house had seen much better days.

★ ★ ★

'Where are we going?' gasped Lenny when they were out of sight of the manor house and Jonas suddenly wheeled about from the direction of the orchards and headed towards the shore. 'You've to go and help your dad!'

'So I will, but I'll see you home first,' he muttered, running out across the shore meadows, slowing as the pair weaved through the plantation and crested the fir-fringed dunes above an old disused boathouse. 'I'll hide here and keep watch till you get indoors,' he said, scanning the curving shoreline towards a jutting headland where Withencroft, the Burfords' long sand-stone house, stood facing the sea. 'There's nobody about, so make a run for it quick. Hang on.' He rubbed at a grimy patch on Lenny's cheek with his shirt-sleeve. 'Soon as you get in, you'd best wash your face before Granny Burford sees you.'

Lenny sighed and nodded. 'See you tomorrow?'

'Aye. No!' groaned Jonas. 'I've to cart

a load of stones up to the marl pits. It'll have to be the next day. Our usual place — the lightning bole in Boyo's Wood?'

'Aye!' Lenny broke from the cover of the plantation, looking back and grinning widely. 'Thanks for showing me the manor house. I'm glad your sister didn't catch us!'

★ ★ ★

Rachel Warmsley would have been very surprised indeed to see her brother's new pal running like a deer from the wind-bowed scrubby firs and scrambling down to the ramshackle boathouse. Once inside, Lenny hastily shed the broad-brimmed hat, and a cascade of chestnut curls fell about her shoulders. A few minutes later, the patched hand-me-downs were safely hidden away for another day, and Eleanor Burford was smoothing down the folds of a clean dress and pinafore, tying a ribbon about her unruly curls before emerging from the boathouse and starting along the damp shore.

Chancing a glance up to the plantation, whence Jonas gave their secret owl-hoot signal, Lenny turned onto a steep sandy path and quickened her step towards Withencroft.

★   ★   ★

Spring was blooming into early summer, and the misty morning boded well for a fine day. Singing softly, Rachel slid a final tray of spiced fruity Founder's Day farls into the oven. She was wrapping cooled batches into muslin when the heavy tramp of boots echoed along the stone passageway. Her father and Edward came into the kitchen. Ben Warmsley glowered at the array of baking, saying nothing.

'Will you be coming with me to Founder's Day, Pa?'

'Every year you ask the same,' returned Ben testily. 'Every year t'answer's same! That free school was your ma's doing. I'm willing to let you carry it on for her sake, but I'll have no part in it. Never have, never will.' With that, he put on his hat and strode outdoors.

Edward paused as he passed by his elder sister, meeting her eyes sympathetically. 'I hope you have a good day at the school, Rachel,' he murmured, adding, 'I daresay Leach will be there, putting in his two penn'orth as usual?'

'Fred Leach's never missed a chance to condemn our school, even when Ma was here,' she replied briskly. 'But Founder's Day is a very special occasion, and I shan't let Fred Leach or any other nay-sayers spoil it.'

'Nevertheless,' said Edward seriously, 'I'm glad Hugh Armstrong's going with you today.'

'It *will* be nice not to be there on my own.' Rachel's pale face coloured slightly, and she smiled shyly across at her brother. 'Afterwards, we're going down to Liverpool and spending the afternoon with Hugh's family at Riverslie House. His uncle is visiting from

America and I'm to meet him.'

'You're really keen on Hugh Armstrong, aren't you?'

'Yes, I am.'

They'd started walking out at Christmastide. She and Hugh had been acquainted for years; he and Agnes's elder brother Tom were old friends, and Hugh often stayed with the Whiteheads, so his and Rachel's paths occasionally crossed in the village. However it wasn't until last December, when Colonel and Mrs Whitehead invited Rachel to a Christmas concert and he was amongst the festive party, that Hugh Armstrong had asked if he might call on Rachel at Pedlars Down.

'I still can't quite believe it,' she confided softly. 'I've always longed to meet somebody, and I dearly want children and a home of my own. But after Ma died and the years went by, I hardly dared hope . . . Then Hugh came courting. I've never been happier, Edward!'

'I'm glad,' he replied warmly. 'You

always work so very hard, Rachel, looking after us and the house and the village and Ma's school — and you've done that ever since Ma first fell ill and you started nursing her. It's high time you had something for yourself,' finished Edward, cocking an ear as Ben bellowed for him to get a move on. 'Nobody deserves happiness more.'

* * *

'So,' said Hugh Armstrong as they set off from the manor house, 'tell me about this Founder's Day of yours.'

'Didn't you have Founder's Day,' teased Rachel, her hazel eyes dancing, 'at that fancy boarding school you, Agnes's brother and the Burford boys went to?'

'We did. I recall it as a grim experience.' Hugh grinned sidelong at her. 'We certainly were never treated to spiced buns by an exceedingly pretty young lady!'

Rachel ignored the compliment, but

was beaming as she said, 'My mother Mariah wasn't a local girl. She'd grown up in Cumbria, attended school and had a good education. When she married Pa and came to Pedlars Down, she was appalled our village didn't have a school, nor was there a school anywhere for miles around. So she set about founding a free school so local children might learn to read, write and cast accounts.'

'An ambitious enterprise indeed,' remarked Hugh. 'What did the village elders make of *that* little idea?'

'Although Ma was respected because she was Squire Warmsley's wife, she was treated like a stranger — an incomer wanting to change age-old village ways and bring in fancy new notions. She never gave up trying to persuade folk about the importance of education, but it was years before Mr and Mrs Leach offered the land and Lane End Cottage for her school. John Leach was a wealthy, influential man, and the village elders had little choice but to agree.' Rachel frowned slightly. 'My mother furnished the cottage and started teaching, but was sorely grieved only boys were permitted to attend — the village elders wouldn't hear of educating girls. Until the end of her days, Ma strove to change their minds.'

'Your mother sounds an ardent reformer,' remarked Hugh, eyeing the laden baskets of baking. 'We appear to be carrying sufficient buns — I beg your pardon, *farls* — to nourish a small army. Do you really need so many?'

'We have lots of pupils this year,' laughed Rachel. 'And boys are always hungry!'

'Ah! And the little parcel of books?' queried Hugh wryly, indicating the package on Rachel's lap.

'Prizes for those boys who have worked hard and tried their best.'

Even as she spoke, Rachel's spirits sank. For as Hugh drove over the ford into the village, Fred Leach, half-brother of the free school's late benefactor, strode toward them, effectively blocking the chaise's way to the school, where the pupils stood waiting in a neat line.

'Look at 'em,' sneered Fred Leach loudly, jerking a thumb in the direction of the poorly clad boys. 'See any future physics or attorneys in that bunch?'

'Mr Leach, I — '

'What use is schooling the likes of them?' he cut in. 'Lads who'll be ploughing fields or digging ditches their whole life? I'm a fair-minded man, and I never baulk at paying my share of dues to this village, but what I cannot abide — and I'm not alone in this as you well know, Miss Warmsley — is squandering hard-earned brass for a school that's neither use nor ornament. Year after year I said the same to your mam, and she'd not listen to sense neither.'

'Enough, sir!' admonished Hugh sharply, glaring distastefully down at the irate man. 'You'll mind your tongue when speaking to a lady!'

'Mr Armstrong, I meant no disrespect.' Fred Leach quickly inclined his head, moving from the chaise's path. 'But what's true is true, sir. That school is a millstone round the neck of this village!'

Hugh drove on at pace, and Rachel sighed heavily. 'The school's always had its share of nay-sayers, but Fred Leach has a particular axe to grind. He's also a loudmouth and a bully.'

'The man's an uncouth character and no mistake,' reflected Hugh, drawing up before the school and its assembled pupils. 'However, there is logic in his argument, Rachel. What benefit is there in educating boys destined to follow their fathers and forefathers into the fields, mills, quarries and so on? Surely that education can only make such boys restless and discontent with their lot?'

'Hugh.' Rachel spun around, her eyes wide in astonishment.

Before she could utter another word, the village schoolmaster hurried forward, a warm smile of welcome on his kindly face, and the Founder's Day celebrations began.

* * *

Riverslie House stood on the high ground, far above the clamour of Liverpool town and the dark, congested river from which the Armstrongs and most other residents of the elegant villas curving along Mersey Brow made and maintained their fortune.

Since she and Hugh had been courting, Rachel had visited Riverslie House upon several occasions, and from the very first was warmly welcomed into the family home by Hugh's parents, Samuel and Elizabeth, and his three brothers and their wives. Although Rachel scarcely remembered it, she'd once met Mr Armstrong years ago. He'd visited Pedlars Down to see Pa and pay his respects shortly after the death of Rachel's mother.

Whenever she entered Riverslie House, Rachel was conscious of being enveloped by wealth, luxury and comfort; drawn into a way of life very different to anything she'd known. And yet with Hugh at her side, she felt completely at home.

'Uncle Harry sailed for America when he was several years younger than I am now,' Hugh was explaining as they went through the spacious flower-filled drawing-room. Its small-paned French doors were thrown open onto a broad terrace, with the heady fragrance and vibrant colours of the rose garden beyond.

'Harry Armstrong's only capital were his wits, sheer determination to succeed and a huge amount of courage,' expounded Hugh, taking Rachel's arm and leading her down to the garden, where the entire family was already gathered in a melee of voices, laughter and small children playing. 'As you'll soon discover, my uncle is a quite exceptional man!'

* * *

After a sumptuous tea, with more varieties of cake and pastries than Rachel could imagine, the party enjoyed a sunny, convivial afternoon in the rose garden until a summer downpour sent everyone scurrying indoors.

The drawing-room was immediately a flurry of activity as entertainments were organised. Several ladies were at the pianoforte choosing music and songs, others settled with needlework or netting, Hugh and his brothers made much of setting up card-tables while arguing about a cricket match, and Rachel wandered across to the well-stocked bookshelves. She was browsing Mrs Armstrong's collection of novels when Hugh's uncle joined her.

'Miss Rachel, I've been wantin' to ask you about Ben,' said Harry Armstrong, his many years in the American deep south lending his speech a soft, slow timbre. 'How's he doin' these days?'

'He's very well, thank you!' she exclaimed, adding, 'I didn't realise you and my father were friends?'

'Oh, yeah, our paths crossed a lot when we were boys,' said Harry, nodding. 'Although your pa was always more Sam's pal than mine. They were around the same age, y'see. I was five, six years older. Sam wrote me when Ben lost your ma,' reflected the elderly man soberly. 'I was very sorry to hear about your family's loss, Miss Rachel. I kinda 'specially felt for Ben, because I'd lately lost my own wife. Like your ma, she was taken far too young.' He expelled a slow breath. 'For a lot of years, I was the loneliest man on the face of this earth. Then I met Lottie, and found somebody to love again,' Harry concluded simply, his eyes meeting Rachel's. 'She was widowed with two young 'uns, so now I have a fine son and a daughter as smart as she is pretty.'

'I'm happy to hear that,' responded Rachel sincerely, returning the warmth of his smile. 'Are your wife and children come to Liverpool with you?'

He shook his head. 'Lottie's a real homebody, and we didn't care for taking the young 'uns on such a long sea voyage. So although it's swell being in England a spell, I'm kinda itching to get back aboard a ship bound for Charleston.'

'You enjoy living in America, then?'

'Surely do! It's home — ' Harry broke off, turning when the muted conversation around the Armstrong brothers' card game erupted into derisive laughter and jeers. Hugh rose from the table, grinning widely and triumphantly brandishing his winnings.

'Looks like their game's over,' commented Harry cheerfully. 'And your young man's the winner! I'm getting to know my nephews, and Hugh impresses me a lot. He has a sharp eye for business, and being the youngest of four brothers realises he must carve out his own place in the family company. He'll do it, too,' he concluded with satisfaction. 'I reckon that boy has a fine future ahead of him. A very fine future indeed!'

★　★　★

'How long will you be, lass?' grumbled Ben Warmsley, the reins loose in his hands as the sturdy black pony drew the wagon away from the flour mill and along the winding track towards Pedlars Down village. 'I've no patience for sitting around while womenfolk dawdle and gossip.'

'I'll be however long it takes to do the errands, Pa,' explained Rachel evenly, running her eye down a lengthy list. 'As well as the groceries and collecting your new boots from the cobbler, I'm taking another basket round to Mrs Silcox because she's still poorly. Agnes has asked me to visit Reverend Greenhalgh this afternoon. She and her mother do keep an eye on him, but he doesn't eat properly. I've baked him a pie,' concluded Rachel absently, consulting the list once more. 'I must call at the Fletcher farm, too.'

'Why?' queried Ben crossly, frowning as the wagon splashed across the ford. 'Why are you visiting the Fletchers? Strapping great bunch! Surely they're not poorly? Or has the whole village been stricken?'

'There may well be seven Fletchers, robust to a man as far as I'm aware,' replied Rachel briskly, snapping shut her bag. 'But not one of them came up to the house and paid their rent this morning. That's the reason I'm calling — unless you'd prefer to do it?'

'You know fine well I've no time for that kind of thing,' Ben returned, shaking his head. 'I always left collecting rents, bookwork and such to your ma. And where's Edward taken himself off to?' he grumbled, clamping his teeth around the stem of a clay pipe. 'No sooner had he brought in the 'tater-cart than he went out again!' Stiffly craning his neck, Ben glanced into the wagon-bed where Jonas was stretched out amongst the sacks of flour, his dog fast asleep beside him. 'Did Edward say owt to you about where he was going?'

'Uh-huh,' yawned the boy, leaning comfortably against the sacks, a wide-brimmed hat tilted down to shade his closed eyes from the bright sunlight. 'Haven't seen him, Pa.'

'If Edward was carrying books,' Rachel ventured as the wagon trundled around the duck pond, 'he's likely returning them to Mr Greenhalgh.'

'But that were hours ago!' protested Ben in exasperation. 'Surely he can't still be jawing about books to the parson?'

'I expect Edward's helping Mr Greenhalgh write his sermon,' she replied.

'We'll be out all day at this carry-on!' Ben expelled a long-suffering breath. 'What's Edward doing writing sermons, anyhow? Why can't Amos Greenhalgh write his own sermons?'

'He's broken his spectacles. Stop over there, Pa!' declared Rachel as they approached St. Cuthbert's. 'By the horse trough, so Billy can have a good drink while I do the errands. Jonas,' she went on, descending from the wagon, 'make yourself useful by taking those tools to the smithy.'

Before Rachel could finish, Rupert's

head shot up; and with a bloodcurdling howl of sheer delight, the pup leapt from the wagon. Jonas sat bolt upright. There was only one person in the whole world Rupert greeted like that — Lenny! Sure enough, his dog was streaking towards Lenny and Grandma Burford crossing the green. 'Rupert!' he yelled, scrambling after him. 'Come here, boy!'

As was customary whenever their paths crossed in the village, Jonas and Lenny pretended not to know one another. Lenny simply bent to stroke the big pup as he gambolled about her, gazing up with adoration in his huge brown eyes.

'Why, hello!' she said with a smile, glancing from Rupert to Harriet Burford's grimly set features. 'Isn't he a fine puppy, Granny?'

'An unruly beast like that shouldn't be running wild about the village,' snapped Harriet, proceeding briskly across the green. 'Come along, child. Don't dawdle!'

At the church corner, Rachel paused

with Reverend Greenhalgh's pie in her hands, waiting so the Burfords might enter the west gate unhindered. She nodded politely. 'Mrs Burford.'

'Rachel,' responded the older woman, inclining her head before pushing open the gate and continuing stiff-backed towards St. Cuthbert's, her arms filled with flowers to be placed before the Burford family's stained-glass memorial window.

Standing with the parson's pie, Rachel expelled an exasperated breath. Harriet Burford had walked at arm's length from Ben Warmsley as if he didn't exist. For his part, Ben, seated up on the wagon, stared straight ahead, ignoring Harriet as she passed by. Turning into the parsonage, Rachel tutted in annoyance. The bitterness between their families never failed to vex her. Surely, after years of distrust and hostility, it was high time bygones were left to be bygones?

* * *

'Such finery!' exclaimed Rachel softly, standing before the glass in her room at Pedlars Down and gazing at herself wearing the graceful ball dress she and Agnes had spent the past month cutting, sewing and trimming. 'I don't look like me at all!'

They had copied the pattern from a plate Agnes spotted in the *Lancashire Ladies' Journal*. The gown was in the Empire style with a full, flowing skirt, gathered sleeves and a becoming square neckline delicately embroidered with beaded tracery. The material was finest layered muslin in pastel mint-green, and had been a gift from Agnes.

'I can't thank you enough for this,' Rachel said, turning to the fashionable younger woman. 'I could barely afford those silk dancing slippers, much less a ball dress! But for your kindness, I wouldn't be able to go to Riverslie House this evening.'

'Thanks are quite unnecessary! As you know, that material's been in my linen chest a twelvemonth and longer,' replied Agnes amiably. 'I bought it on impulse but it really isn't my colour, whereas it suits you to perfection. You look lovely — and you must be so excited!'

'I'm nervous,' confided Rachel, moving from the glass and taking the deckle-edged invitation from her dresser. 'It's such a grand occasion — *Mr and Mrs Samuel Armstrong's Annual Ball in aid of the Liverpool Merchants' Benevolent Fund for War Widows and Orphans.* All the town's great and good will be present, including the Lord Mayor himself! I don't want to let Hugh, or his family, down.'

'You won't,' insisted Agnes confidently. 'Once you arrive on Hugh's arm, you'll have a splendid evening.'

Rachel looked doubtful. 'I'm familiar with the country dances and reels, but if a cotillion is called, I shall — '

'Dance it beautifully!' declared the irrepressible Agnes. 'The changes are quite standard, and we've been practising those. You'll easily pick up any

34

variations.' She paused before adding guilelessly, 'Has Hugh asked to speak to your father?'

Rachel flushed to the roots of her dark hair, quite lost for words.

Agnes laughed. 'Hugh Armstrong is being extremely attentive! Coming often to Pedlars Down, taking you driving, accompanying you to church . . . Village folk are talking.'

'Folk always gossip.'

'Hugh is such a catch!' cried Agnes. 'Wealthy, accomplished, handsome too. You're the envy of every spinster in the county! So, pray, when may I expect to wish you happiness?'

Rachel shook her head, embarrassed and exasperated at her romantic friend's persistence. 'Hugh hasn't even hinted at an engagement.'

'Not yet,' retorted Agnes blithely. 'But then, he hasn't seen you in this dress!'

* * *

In the heat of a sultry August night, the sweeping drive of Riverslie House was lit with flickering lanterns and lined with shining carriages as honoured guests continued arriving. Within, all was excitement and anticipation, for as well as being patrons of many good causes, Samuel and Elizabeth Armstrong were renowned as the most convivial and hospitable of hosts.

It was they who called the first dance of the evening, selecting a tune, and with much merriment choosing the figures for an especially vigorous country dance, which required a deal of agile stepping, skipping and hand-clapping.

Rachel took her place in the long lines of dancers and stood facing Hugh, her heart beating fast and her dainty silk dancing slippers feeling heavier than lead. However, when Mr and Mrs Armstrong led off from the top, progressing down the line, and the other couples began dancing, Rachel quite forgot her nerves. Hugh was a confident, accomplished partner, and she felt lighter than thistledown as they danced together down the progression. The second dance was duly called, even livelier and more intricate than the first. Swept along by the music and the heady pleasure of holding Hugh's hand, touching his shoulder, feeling his arm about her waist as they stepped and circled, met and parted, turned about and came together, Rachel had never been happier.

After the set ended, Hugh was leading her from the floor when his eldest brother signalled his attention from the doorway. 'I must have a word with George,' murmured Hugh, approaching the chairs where George Armstrong's wife Adele was seated. 'Will you excuse me, my dear?'

Rachel took a seat beside Adele, who muttered, 'Just look at them!'

In the doorway, Hugh and George were being joined by their remaining brothers.

'You'll get used to this, Rachel,' went

on Adele. 'Those four work side by side every day. Yet whenever they meet at a social gathering, sooner or later they end up in a corner together talking about cotton. It's always business with Armstrong men,' she added in vexation. 'Business, business — oh, no!' Adele broke off at the sight of a large jovial man approaching. 'Mr Watson is pleasant enough, but dancing is definitely *not* his forte. Still, one mustn't refuse . . . ' She was duly led into the dance, and Rachel was left alone only a few moments before Harry Armstrong joined her.

'I hear there's punch somewhere,' he said genially, offering his arm. 'Shall we track it down?'

They found the huge crystal punch-bowl and took their cups through to the high-ceiled loggia. It was cool and softly lit, with several other guests already seated there conversing quietly.

'I'm not sure what's in this punch,' remarked Harry. 'We'd call it firewater back home.'

Rachel smiled. 'Why did you go to America all those years ago, Mr Armstrong?'

'Necessity.' He shrugged. 'Sam and I were doing all right here in Liverpool, but we knew we'd do a whole lot better if one of us was over in cotton country.'

'It's such an enormous decision.'

'It was a *wise* decision,' he said simply. 'Armstrong's is thriving there. You know, Miss Rachel, I was truly taken aback when Hugh told me he wanted to come work with me in Charleston, but I was more than happy to agree. Hugh's an enterprising young man who . . . ' The elderly man plainly believed she knew about Hugh's plans, and continued discussing the move.

Shocked, Rachel couldn't believe what she was hearing. This could not be! Collecting herself as best she could, she presently made polite excuses and quit the loggia.

Weaving through the crush of guests, she reached the dimly lit, deserted drawing-room. Its French doors were open onto the terrace. Despite the heat of the night, Rachel felt chilled to the bone as she stood there alone, heedless of time passing.

'Here you are, my dear!' exclaimed Hugh exuberantly, striding onto the terrace. 'I've been searching.'

Rachel turned, confronting him. 'When,' she said calmly, quite composed now, 'did you intend telling me you're leaving for America?'

2

'Hugh's leaving for America?' echoed Edward Warmsley in disbelief, turning sharply from digging in the kitchen garden. 'And you didn't find out until his uncle told you last night at the Armstrongs' ball?'

'It was such a shock . . . I couldn't believe it,' confided Rachel unhappily, her head bowed as she knelt tending the bed of herbs. 'When I confronted Hugh and he told me it was true, all I wanted was to come home and be by myself,' she went on, reliving those dreadful moments at Riverslie House. 'But of course I couldn't, not without making a fuss. And I didn't want to offend Mr and Mrs Armstrong, so — so Hugh and I stayed,' Rachel faltered, memories rushing back of dancing with him at the end of the night, all the while realising it would be the very last time she'd feel

Hugh's arms about her. 'Hugh's clearly elated at the prospect of going to America,' she concluded briskly, straightening up and starting indoors. 'He said he'll call on me later today.'

★　★　★

Hugh Armstrong arrived at Pedlars Down that afternoon, immediately presenting Rachel with an enormous bouquet of fragrant floribunda roses. 'I'm afraid I can't claim praise for these flowers,' he said genially as Rachel took them from him. 'They're from Mother — she said you particularly admired this variety when you and she were in the rose garden together.'

'Yes, I did,' replied Rachel softly, raising her face from the velvety petals to glance at Hugh. 'They're beautiful. Please do be sure and thank your mother, won't you?'

'I will indeed. And while the roses may not be my doing,' he said with a smile, offering her a neatly wrapped casket of chocolates, 'I *can* take full credit for these — almond creams are your favourites, aren't they?'

Rachel nodded, turning away to place the flowers and chocolates on the dresser. 'Thank you, Hugh.'

'My pleasure. You know, I'm still annoyed that Uncle Harry told you I'd be sailing to the Americas with him,' reflected Hugh, taking a seat in the sunlit compass window as Rachel brought a tray of coffee and set it onto the small circular three-legged table. 'I wanted to tell you the news myself, but I simply didn't have any opportunity.'

'Yes, you said that last night,' Rachel remarked evenly, pouring the hot, strong coffee. 'And how the arrangement with your uncle came about unexpectedly.'

'Practically spontaneously,' returned Hugh affably. 'Uncle Harry was discussing Charleston, and suddenly the opportunity arose. What a splendid opportunity it is too, Rachel!' he enthused. 'A major step in my building a prosperous future 'pon my own account. For while my brothers and I know all there is to know about the cotton trade in Liverpool, I — *I alone* — am about to learn how Harry's Charleston company works!' He gazed over to Rachel expectantly, and after a moment when she didn't respond, added impatiently, 'Do you not understand how important this is?' Without waiting for her reply, he explained, 'My uncle's getting on in years, Rachel. The day will come when the Charleston company passes to the next generation. Harry doesn't have any children. Not even a daughter whose husband might inherit the company.'

'Your uncle *does* have a family,' interrupted Rachel with a vexed, impatient shake of her head. 'A daughter and a young son! He's told me how very much he's missing them!'

'They're only the children of Harry's second wife,' retorted Hugh dismissively. 'Of course he's fond of them — Harry's that sort of man. But when it comes to inheriting the family company, mark my words, only blood signifies. While I'm in Charleston, I'll discover every last detail about successfully running my uncle's company.' Hugh shrugged, smiling at Rachel above the rim of his coffee cup. 'I'll obviously be Harry's natural successor, and . . .'

Hugh was in full flow, expounding upon the glowing future that surely lay ahead. Rachel could think only that the future *she'd* longed for — dared hope for — was now never to be. Her slender fingers knotted in her lap. Sitting so close to Hugh in the compass window, she barely clung to her composure. Fearing her voice would tremble and betray her feelings, she hardly said a word while Hugh discussed his imminent departure for America. It hurt her deeply that he didn't once speak of their parting. Rachel's heart suddenly lurched. If Hugh knew she loved him, would it make a difference? Would he change his mind and stay in Liverpool?

45

PROPERTY OF MERTHYR TYDFIL PUBLIC LIBRARIES

No, of course he wouldn't. Even in her unhappiness, Rachel was scrupulously fair. Hugh hadn't led her on. There had never been mention of an understanding between them. Naught but Rachel's own foolish fancies had led her to imagine Hugh intended asking her to marry him. At least she'd been spared the humiliation of his realising her expectations. They would simply part as friends.

Presently Hugh rose, and together they walked slowly toward the great oaken door, pausing on the threshold. 'I can't be certain how long I'll be away,' he was saying, turning towards Rachel and taking her slim hands within his own. 'However, you have my solemn promise I'll be a prolific letter-writer!'

'When — ' Treacherously, Rachel's voice failed. 'When exactly are you leaving, Hugh?'

'Oh, this evening,' he answered. 'Harry and I are sailing with the tide.'

'So soon!' Rachel's breath caught in her throat. Her resolve to accept what she could not change crumbled; and when she gazed up at Hugh, her clear hazel eyes betrayed all that was in her heart. 'Then this really is the last time.'

Hugh's brisk mood unexpectedly softened, and he bent to brush her cheek with a kiss. 'During recent months, I've been the happiest of men,' he murmured, drawing her clasped hands to his lips. 'I shall miss you very much.'

'God speed,' whispered Rachel as he turned from her and started down the worn stone steps. 'Fare thee well, Hugh.'

★   ★   ★

In the days and weeks following Hugh's departure, Rachel strove not to dwell upon wistful notions of what might have been. Summer ended, and she sought refuge and comfort in the familiar pattern of daily life as the seasons turned.

Her days were filled with bringing

home the harvest: gathering in the orchard fruit and all the ensuing storing, bottling, jamming and pickling, so provisions might last the long winter through. She and Agnes Whitehead helped Reverend Greenhalgh prepare the music and rehearse the choir for Harvest Thanksgiving at St. Cuthbert's; together with Edward they distributed the traditional alms-baskets to the poor, needy and infirm of the parish. And now, as the days grew shorter and chillier, Rachel was busy making ready the village free school to open its doors for another year. Yesterday she'd made a start whitewashing the stone-built walls inside the schoolhouse, and this morning was relaying pails, mops, brooms and other sundries from the manor house onto a cart already stacked with fallen deadwood.

'You're off to that school again, I see,' grumbled Ben from across the yard. 'Haven't you enough work here to keep you busy?'

'I'll be back in good time for tea,

Pa,' she said mildly. Clambering up into the cart and taking Billy's reins, Rachel drove away from the manor house. Edward was working in the oat field and she slowed alongside, hailing him. 'Have you seen Jonas? I need him at the school to unload this firewood ready for Mr Cumstock's coming home.'

'He went out early,' called Edward. 'Maybe he and his pals are making the most of their last week before school starts.'

'More than likely,' agreed Rachel, reflecting practically. 'Not that many of Jonas's pals attend school. Those few who *were* pupils left in the summer and are working now — I'm surprised they still have time for skylarking with Jonas.'

'I'll come down later to unload and chop the kindling,' Edward offered with an easy smile. 'While I'm there, remind me to fix that shelf in the book cupboard.'

* * *

Eleanor Burford heard Jonas's owl-hoot signal as clear as a bell. She was up in her bright, airy room at Withencroft working on her lessons. Her room was at a corner of the Burfords' long sandstone house and had big windows on two sides, so Eleanor could see two places at once. As well as some of the shore and the old tumbledown boat-house, she also had a fine view of the fir plantation, and knew from the owl-hoot that Jonas was waiting there for her.

She wouldn't be able to nip out until after Granny went visiting, so Eleanor leaned from the window, returned Jonas's hoot and waved wildly with her bonnet — which was the signal to let him know she'd meet him soon. She had no sooner resumed the English exercise Granny had set for her when there was a soft tap at the door and Harriet Burford entered, already done up in hat and gloves and ready to go visiting in the village.

'How are you finding this exercise?' she asked, coming to look at Eleanor's writing tablet. 'My word, you're doing very well! You try hard at everything you do, my dear — that's an admirable quality!'

Eleanor said nothing, but her cheeks glowed with happiness. She'd thought the old grandmother very fierce and quite scary when she and her brother and sister first came to live at Withencroft, but by and by, Eleanor was becoming very fond of Harriet Burford.

'I shan't be long visiting Colonel and Mrs Whitehead, and while I'm away I want you to put on your oldest clothes and be ready.'

Eleanor's jaw dropped. 'What for?'

'It's a beautifully clear day, and wind and tide are perfect,' laughed Harriet, ruffling the girl's shock of chestnut curls. 'I'm going to teach you to sail, young lady!'

Eleanor couldn't wait to tell Jonas. The very instant Harriet's carriage drew away from Withencroft, Eleanor was along the shore to the derelict boathouse. Changing into the disguise she wore whenever she and Jonas met up, she wondered what Granny would say if she wore these old hand-me-downs Jonas had given her when they went sailing that afternoon!

Racing up into the fir plantation, Eleanor was greeted by an overjoyed Rupert and immediately knelt to pat the delighted pup. When she looked up and saw Jonas, however, she gasped in horror. There was blood across his shirt-front, and his face was cut and swelling up beneath one eye. 'What's happened to you?' she demanded, her gaze dropping to his hands and scuffed knuckles. 'Have you been fighting, Jonas?'

'Never mind,' he muttered, grabbing her arm and breaking into a run. 'Let's just go!'

They ran beyond the firs, over the dunes and across the shore fields into the heart of Boyo's Wood, flopping down breathless onto the springy carpet of thick moss and leaning back against the fallen bole of the lightning tree.

'Are you going to tell me?'

'No,' mumbled Jonas sullenly, not looking at her.

'You might as well,' Eleanor said matter-of-factly. 'I'm not going to stop asking.'

For a while, Jonas didn't say anything; merely fished a wedge of plum-bread from his pocket, broke it in half and handed Eleanor the biggest share. They ate in silence.

'I was in the village,' he said awkwardly, stroking Rupert's rough neck, too embarrassed to look Eleanor in the eye. 'Had a set-to with three lads from school.'

She reached up, gently touching his bloody cheek. 'Did you thump 'em back?'

Jonas spun round to face her. 'I couldn't, Lenny!' he almost cried, his eyes wide and tormented. 'How could I? They were younger than me — don't you see?'

'Not really.' She shook her head. 'There were three of them.'

'You don't understand,' he went on

rapidly, raking a bruised hand through his unruly hair. 'Everybody at school is younger than me! It were bad enough last year; it'll be even worse this! Everybody else leaves when they're 11 or 12 — younger, even — and I've already turned 13! It's shamin', Lenny!' blurted Jonas in frustration. 'It's shamin' for a lad my age to be going to school like a bairn!'

'No it's not!' she returned stoutly, adding a tad wistfully, 'I wish *I* was going to school.'

'Girls don't go to school,' commented Jonas absently.

'Not in Pedlars Down, they don't,' returned Eleanor tartly. 'Granny said the lady who started the school wanted it for boys *and* girls, and it's nothing short of a disgrace that this village wouldn't have it then and still won't have it now!'

'Lenny, will you stop mithering on about the school!' he snapped, getting to his feet.

'I went to school in New Brighton,'

she persisted, also scrambling up. 'And I liked it!'

'Aye, well, you're welcome to it,' Jonas muttered irritably, indicating the lengths of driftwood he'd collected and stowed nearby. 'I've brought some tools so we can start the tree-house.'

'I can't — not today. Granny Burford's taking me sailing this afternoon.'

'You'd best be on your way then,' cut in Jonas coldly, his eyes lowered to the mossy ground. 'You'll not want to keep her waiting.'

*   *   *

'Look how little our house looks, Granny!' exclaimed Eleanor, pointing ashore to where Withencroft's reddish-pink sandstone walls were glowing in the strong autumn sunlight, its many windows dazzling like rows of golden squares.

Eleanor was standing at the side, watching land get further and further away as with sails billowing, the boat flew through white-crested waves, leaving a lacy trail in her wake.

Harriet Burford dipped into the big pocket of her coat, offering a small but very well-made nautical instrument to Eleanor, who came hurrying along the deck to join her at the wheel. 'Look through this spy-glass — it makes everything look much bigger!'

'It's like magic!' Eleanor cried, holding the glass to her eye. 'I can even see one of the windows in my room!'

'It used to be *my* room,' laughed Harriet. 'Very long ago.'

'How long have you lived in our house, Granny?' asked Eleanor, her eye still to the spy-glass.

'Always. I was born at Withencroft. My father, Captain Cedric Swann, built the house when he and my mother wed. After I grew up and married, my husband Sydney Burford came to live at Withencroft, and our son David was born there. He was Malcolm and Peter's father.'

'It's a big family, isn't it?' Eleanor mused, smoothing her fingers across the gleaming brass band on the spy-glass. 'Until Madge wed Malcolm, there was just the three of us — me, Madge and Felix — ' She broke off, noticing some fancy lettering engraved into the brass and looking up inquisitively. 'Granny, what's this mean?'

'Ah! Those are my father's and my initials, and the date he gave me that spy-glass,' explained Harriet, her eyes twinkling. 'It was my birthday present, and Papa gave it to me because I loved the sea and sailing every bit as much as he did. I was about your age then,' she finished, smiling at the girl by her side. 'Perhaps you'd like to keep it, Eleanor, to bring with you when we come sailing?'

Eleanor nodded vigorously. 'Thank you, Granny. I'll look after it!'

'I know you will, my dear. If you point your spy-glass over there and look a little way inland — yes, that's it — you'll be able to see the town where

Felix has gone to school.'

Eleanor trained her eye on the landmark. Her younger brother had gone away to boarding school a few days earlier. They'd never been separated before.

'You must miss Felix a lot,' Harriet said gently. 'I'm sorry if you're lonely, Eleanor.'

'Oh, I'm not, Granny! I've got — ' she said, biting her tongue just in time to stop mentioning Jonas Warmsley. 'I — I'm not lonely. Honest, I'm not.'

While they sailed on, following the sweep of the rugged Lancashire coastline, Eleanor's thoughts about Jonas were running from one to the other. 'Granny,' she ventured at length, 'what started the feud between us and the Warmsleys?'

'My goodness!' exclaimed Harriet, taken aback by the blunt question. 'I wouldn't describe it quite so dramatically as a feud, Eleanor. More of a rift between families.'

'What started it, though?'

'The troubles between the Burfords and Warmsleys happened so long ago, I doubt anybody really knows the truth of it,' sighed Harriet. 'The families were related by marriage. As I understand it, two cousins, a Burford and a Warmsley, had dealings together involving land and money. There was a bitter falling-out, the situation became a matter of honour, and the cousins decided to settle it with a wager. I don't know any more about it,' Harriet went on hastily, seeing the wide-eyed Eleanor drawing breath to enquire further. 'Sydney, my husband, would only say the Warmsleys cheated his family. He told me the Burfords were ruined. They lost everything, and were left virtually penniless,' she concluded quietly. 'To the end of his days, Sydney held the Warmsleys responsible for the hardships and suffering his grandfather and father endured.'

'The feud isn't really anything to do with you then, is it?' reasoned Eleanor, once more running her fingers over the inscription on the spy-glass. 'Your family was Swann, not Burford.'

'I married a Burford,' replied Harriet simply. 'I respected and abided by my husband's wishes concerning the Warmsleys, and continue to do so. I owe Sydney's memory my loyalty.'

'Had you got on with Warmsleys before?' persisted Eleanor curiously.

'Our families were friends as well as neighbours,' Harriet reflected, gazing over the glittering waves and steering a steady course along the coast. 'My parents and old Mr and Mrs Warmsley were very close indeed, and Ben Warmsley and I grew up together.'

'But you had to fall out with them after you got wed?'

'Yes.' Harriet smiled sadly, looking down into Eleanor's rosy upturned face. 'Yes, I fell out with the Warmsleys. Now, would you like to take the wheel and steer?'

Eagerly, Eleanor ducked within her grandmother's arms, standing on tiptoe to clasp the big smooth wheel with both hands. 'I can't see where we're going, Granny!'

'I'll be your look-out,' reassured Harriet, her own hands guiding the wheel. 'You're doing fine — steady as she goes!'

Eleanor laughed. She was having a grand day and couldn't wait to tell Jonas all about it. She just hoped Granny never found out about them being pals.

★　★　★

The squat schoolhouse had once been a workshop with an adjoining two-storey cottage. Together with a stable and several out-buildings, it stood on Meadow Well, a sizeable tract of fertile land curving along the river bank and away from the village. Drawing the cart up to the schoolhouse door, Rachel unhitched Billy and, opening the meadow gate, turned the stocky little horse out to graze beneath shady trees while she got on with her chores.

Leaving the schoolhouse door wide open to the crisp autumnal air, Rachel set to finishing the whitewashing. Some while later, she surveyed her handiwork with satisfaction. There were still the small-paned windows to wash and the floor to be sanded, but once those were done she could prepare the cottage for Mr Cumstock's return that evening.

Picking up a clean pail, Rachel started outdoors to draw water from the pump, stopping in her tracks on the threshold. Fred Leach was standing out there. The burly farmer was leaning with his arms folded along the top of the meadow gate, just standing there, looking straight across at the schoolhouse's open door.

Rachel was startled, unaccountably threatened by Leach's presence. How long had he been there? Was he spying on her? Drawing a steadying breath, she stepped from the schoolhouse and strode towards him. Fred Leach pushed himself back from the gate and eyed her.

'Can I help you, Mr Leach?' she enquired curtly.

'By rights, Meadow Well is my land and this is my property. Your ma knew it, and so do you.' His thick lips curled into a sneer as he sauntered past her towards the inn, adding over his shoulder, 'You can think on that while you're fixing up your little school!'

Rachel watched him disappear into Millers Inn, expelling a relieved breath. Fred Leach had been dead-set against the free school since its very beginning, and even now, all these years later, never missed any chance to stir up trouble. She hoped she'd seen the last of him for today at least, and hurried through to the cottage where schoolmaster Ernest Cumstock lived. However, while Rachel swept, dusted and polished the small neat rooms, she couldn't shake off her unease about Leach, and was heartened at hearing Agnes Whitehead's cheery hello from the schoolhouse door.

'I'm in here, Agnes!' she called from the cottage.

A moment later, Agnes appeared in the tiny parlour carrying a large parcel, which she immediately began unwrapping. 'I spotted Billy and guessed you'd be preparing for Mr Cumstock's homecoming. Can you use these curtains? They're from our guest room. Mama's redecorating and choosing new ones,' concluded Agnes, offering the bundle. 'Will they do?'

'They're fine!' exclaimed Rachel, admiring the weight and quality of the patterned curtains. 'This material will really keep out the draughts.'

'Mr Cumstock won't be offended, will he?' asked Agnes, the silk flowers on her fashionable bonnet bobbing as she spoke. 'He's such a kindly old gentleman, I wouldn't want to hurt his feelings.'

'I'm sure he'll appreciate your kindness,' reassured Rachel, looking at the cottage's thin, faded curtains which had clearly seen better days. 'Truth to tell,

Mr Cumstock keeps this cottage as clean and tidy as a box of new pins, but he doesn't pay much attention to home comforts.'

'Poor man, living all alone,' sighed Agnes sympathetically, helping hold the new curtains against the windows to get a measurement. 'I'm glad he's able to stay with his daughter during school vacations . . . Rachel,' she went on after a moment, her bright blue eyes filled with concern as she looked sidelong at her friend, 'how are you getting along? *Really*, I mean?'

'I'm not sure. Some days are better than others,' confided Rachel at length. 'I have so many blessings and much to be thankful for, and sometimes I think I'm getting along quite well with everything. After all, I have Pa and the boys and the household depending on me, and my responsibilities in the village and here at Ma's school. But I miss Hugh more than words can say, Agnes! I still love him, and sometimes the sadness and — and *emptiness* of being without him is almost unbearable,' she whispered, her hand flying to her lips as her voice faltered. 'I long to see him, hear his voice, be with Hugh again.'

Agnes rested a comforting hand upon the older woman's slender shoulder. 'I suppose it's far too soon for a letter from him?' she ventured gently. 'Hugh did promise to write often, didn't he?'

'I believe the ship will be at sea for some weeks yet,' replied Rachel practically, gaining a firm grip on her fragile emotions. 'Besides, I can hardly expect Hugh to abide by that promise. When he arrives in Charleston, he'll be busy settling in and taking up his duties with his uncle's company. It's such a long and perilous voyage, Agnes,' she fretted thoughtfully. 'Thousands of miles of treacherous ocean to cross . . . I pray Hugh reaches America safe and sound.'

'I'm sure he will,' was all Agnes could think to reply, adding, 'And I'm sure Hugh *will* write to you, the very moment he sets foot ashore.'

Rachel nodded, considering the curtains once more. 'I'll be able to alter these and put them up by tonight.'

'Oh, is it this evening Mr Cumstock's coming back?'

'Edward's meeting him from the stagecoach,' replied Rachel warmly. She and her brother regarded Ernest Cumstock as a very dear friend. He had taught their mother Mariah at the village school in Cumbria where she'd grown up, and at her request had come out of retirement to teach at Pedlars Down when Mariah opened her free school.

'And of course, we're eating together this evening,' Rachel went on with a smile, for having supper at the cottage to welcome the elderly schoolmaster home from his travels had become a custom the friends looked forward to. 'It'll be grand having Mr Cumstock back — we miss him!'

★　★　★

It was late when the stagecoach trundled into the village and clattered to a halt outside Millers Inn, where Edward was waiting. While Mr Cumstock stood a moment, easing the stiffness from his joints, Edward gathered together his baggage and indicated a handbill newly posted outside the inn. Mr Cumstock moved closer to read it, frowning as he did so.

The night was chill, with a persistent mizzle; and when Rachel opened the door and drew Ernest Cumstock into the warm, welcoming cottage, she immediately saw how cold and weary the elderly man looked after his long journey from the Midlands. The bright crackling fire and a hot toddy gradually revived him; and when they gathered around the supper table, conversation between the friends soon turned to the perennial worry about whether sufficient pupils would be attending the free school this year.

'Jonas will likely be the eldest boy in school,' remarked Rachel, aware her brother had little taste for schooling at the best of times, much less when his pals had already left and found jobs. 'He doesn't have much enthusiasm for learning, I'm afraid.'

'Jonas is an intelligent boy,' said Mr Cumstock mildly. 'But, like many boys, he needs to apply himself. If Jonas puts his mind to it, he'll surely win a scholarship to Hardwick — just as you did, Edward.'

'It was easier for me,' responded Edward quietly. 'I'm a bookworm, as Ma was, but Jonas is cut from different cloth. He's more like Pa. Book-learning comes hard for him.'

'Aye, that's true enough. Jonas hasn't been happy at school for some while,' sighed the elderly man, pausing a moment before turning to Rachel and continuing reluctantly. 'Edward showed me a handbill Fred Leach has put up outside the inn. He's taking on labour at the quarry. Leach has boys as young as eight working for him up there, and the prospect of regular wages is a powerful reason for needy families to take their sons out of school and put them to work.'

'Which will suit Fred Leach's purposes down to the ground,' muttered Rachel, setting warm apple and blackberry cobbler and a jug of creamy vanilla sauce on the table. 'I wouldn't put any foul trick beyond him!'

Edward picked up on his sister's tone of voice and looked sharply at her. 'Has he been bothering you while you've been here at the schoolhouse?'

'Nothing out of the ordinary,' Rachel dismissed, but frowned in agitation. 'The man already owns every other stick and stone of his late brother's farm and quarry — why on earth does he persist fighting to close down Ma's school and insist Meadow Well is rightfully his?'

'To his way of thinking, the land this school stands on was stolen from his inheritance,' reasoned Mr Cumstock soberly. 'Since the reading of his brother's will, he's vowed to get

Meadow Well back, and I fear Fred Leach won't be still until he succeeds. Old grudges die hard, Miss Warmsley.'

∗ ∗ ∗

On the morning of the new term, breakfast was long since eaten and cleared. Rachel was greasing pudding basins while keeping an eye on a simmering stew-pot, and about to call Jonas for the umpteenth time when she heard his boots clumping down the stair.

'Let me have a look at you,' she said, setting aside a basin when he trailed into the kitchen. 'You'll do. Here's your snap-tin for dinnertime. Off you go, then!'

Jonas shoved the tin into his pocket and took the tea-can Rachel handed him without a word, pausing to pat Rupert, who was stretched out on the rag rug by the door.

'Look lively,' chivvied Rachel impatiently, 'or you'll be late on your first day back!'

Jonas trudged from the manor house

without a backward glance, dawdling on the long walk down towards the village. When he finally got to Meadow Well, the schoolhouse door was shut. Mr Cumstock must've already rung the bell and the boys had gone in.

Jonas hesitated. He hadn't wanted to come to school at all, but now that he had, he certainly didn't fancy going in late with everybody staring at him. In a flash he made up his mind, haring through the village and away before anybody could see him or stop him. He headed inland, dodging out of sight beyond the bank whenever he spotted one of the quarry wagons bearing down the old drovers' track towards the Liverpool-bound road.

Keeping close to trees and hedgerows as much as he could, Jonas was forced out onto open land when he came to Leach's sprawling farm. The main gates were wide open and a cowman was driving the herd into the yard. Leach himself and another man emerged from one of the sheds, haggling over something if the snatches of talk Jonas heard were anything to go by. He ducked out of sight until they'd gone, then veered across country towards Greywethers. Hidden by woods and tucked away amongst neglected gardens, the big old house had been empty for years and was the perfect place for Jonas to hide out. However, as the day wore on, he started brooding on what Pa and Rachel would do when they found out he'd skipped school, and about having to go back there tomorrow. Heavy-footed, he began the long walk home.

Approaching Leach's farm, Jonas spotted several cottagers from Pedlars Down huddled around a handbill nailed to the gatepost. Aiming to sidle past unnoticed, he quickened his pace, but one of the men saw him and called out.

'Good day, Master Warmsley. Will ye come and read this 'un for us?'

Jonas did as he was bidden.

'Bah, it's only young 'uns Leach is

wantin',' cackled one of the men, who was ninety if he was a day. 'No point *me* fetchin' up to the quarry!'

'Nor none of us, neither,' agreed another, turning away from the hand-bill. 'But I'll pass t'word on to my daughter. She's got a couple of bairns and could do with 'em bringin' some brass home.'

Jonas lingered at the handbill while the cottagers went on their way, and was about to make a move himself when he heard the crunch of boots on gravel and spun around to see Fred Leach striding purposefully towards him.

'Aye, yon's right enough, young Warmsley! I'm looking for them as'll do a day's work for a day's pay,' he announced loudly. 'You're a big strong lad, and I've seen you working with your brother and your pa. I know you can put your back into a job, so I'd not hesitate in taking you on.'

Jonas stared at him. 'You're offering me a job — for proper wages and such?'

'More than that, lad — I'm offering you independence. A lad like you doesn't want to be a schoolboy tied to your sister's apron strings — not when you could be doing a man's job for a man's wage.'

Jonas stared at the handbill with fresh eyes, notions of money and freedom and no more school whirling around his mind.

'I've not got all day, lad,' finished Leach amiably. 'Take it or leave it — which'll it be?'

3

Jonas's heart was hammering, his thoughts churning as, with his hands thrust deep into his breech pockets, he strode apace from Fred Leach's gate.

He was no fool. Like everybody else in Pedlars Down, Jonas had heard plenty about how hard a master Fred Leach was. Quarrymen said he had a foul temper, and when Leach cracked the whip you jumped to it or you were out on your ear with no job — and not a farthing of any wages owing to be paid, neither.

There were accidents up at the quarry, too. Some bad 'uns and all. A fuse-man had been killed a year or so back. Folk said it was Leach's fault — that he cut corners, pushing his men into risking their necks so he could make bigger profits. Aye, Jonas well knew all of that! He shook his head impatiently. *He* wouldn't be scared off by the hard graft or the danger. Accidents were bound to happen in a quarry. Working for Leach meant Jonas would be his own man at last. And the wages on offer meant far more brass than he'd ever held in the palm of his hand. Independence and the brass to go with it. His for the taking!

Jonas slowed his pace, expelling a measured breath. Rachel was bound to fly off the handle when she found out what he'd done today. No matter what he said, she'd never understand why taking Leach up on his offer meant so much to him. But Jonas reckoned Pa would see things his way. Pa never paid any mind to the school and book-learning.

Light was fading when Jonas reached Pedlars Down. School was finished for the day and the lads long since gone home. Passing by the schoolhouse, however, Jonas could see old Cumstock pottering about inside, tidying up and such. About to keep his head down and walk on, Jonas faltered, puffing out his cheeks.

When he got home, he'd have to own up to what he'd done and face his sister's sharp tongue and take whatever punishment she dished out. Most likely even more chores, figured Jonas morosely, and never taking her eyes off him so he couldn't sneak off to meet Lenny in Boyo's Wood anymore.

There was no shirking it. He'd best get on with it, and start by setting things straight with Cumstock. Exhaling a resigned breath, Jonas aimed the scuffed toe of his boot at a stone and sent it skittering. Turning about, he trailed back to the schoolhouse and knocked on the closed door.

★　★　★

Rupert's joyful barking rang out from the manor house long before Jonas's boots scraped on the worn stone step and he shoved open the heavy kitchen door. With the pup gambolling round his legs, all ears and tail and licks, Jonas went inside and found Rachel where he expected to find her, there in the kitchen making supper.

'You're late,' she remarked without looking round from stirring an earthenware pot simmering on the hob.

'Aye,' mumbled Jonas, straightening up from patting Rupert and hovering in the centre of the hot kitchen. He cleared his throat. 'I didn't go to school today.'

'I know,' was all she said.

'Oh.' He crossed the flagged stone floor, dragging out a chair and sitting at the table.

'You can't stay there! I need the table now. Go over to the settle if you want to sit down,' said Rachel, fetching a trug of carrots and a string of onions from the pantry.

'How did you know I didn't go to school?' he returned, taken aback.

'I looked in at the school before dinnertime. You weren't there.'

Jonas frowned. 'Old Cumstock said

nowt about that!'

'Have you seen Mr Cumstock?' she queried sharply. 'When?'

'Just now. I've just come from there.'

Rachel didn't pause from peeling onions and scraping carrots; simply allowed her headstrong young brother to have his say. 'Are you certain about this decision, Jonas?' she asked when his words finally dried up. 'You do understand you'll have to see it through? There can be no shilly-shallying, not once you've given your word.'

'I know that, Rachel,' he glowered. 'And I've already given my word. I promised Cumstock I'll be back at school tomorrow morning. I'll not break my promise.'

'Then I'm proud of you.' Crossing to the settle, Rachel rested a reddened work-worn hand on his shoulder. 'You've done the right thing, Jonas.'

'Have I?' he demanded bitterly. 'Right for who? Oh aye, I turned down Leach's job right enough — walked away from it. But I *wanted* that job!

Wanted it more than anything in the world! I don't give two hoots about books and I can't abide schooling. I'm not a bairn anymore. I want to do a man's work for a man's pay — can you not understand that, Rachel?'

Rising from the settle and with Rupert at his side, the boy made for the steep, crooked stairs leading up from the back kitchen. Pausing at the foot, he spun around to face Rachel, his eyes and his fury cold as ice. 'I don't remember our ma at all — not even what her face looked like. But that school was *her* school. *Ma's* school. I couldn't go over to Fred Leach's side. I'm no turncoat, Rachel. But make no mistake — that's the only reason I didn't grab that job with both hands. If another opportunity ever comes my way, I'll be off and gone like a shot!'

* * *

Eleanor stared through the carriage window as the high-stepping grey horses clattered through Liverpool's maze of narrow, teeming streets. It was her first ever visit to the town, and it was bigger, busier, smokier, noisier, darker and far, far more crowded than anything she could have imagined.

Then the Burford carriage rounded a corner, rattling over cobbles and down onto the waterfront. The cramped grimy streets and towering soot-blackened buildings vanished from sight. Opening up before her were sky and water and ships — more ships than Eleanor could count, crammed like pins in a box all along the quaysides. And there were hundreds and hundreds of people, the like of whom she hadn't known or seen before. Every last one of them seemed to be in the greatest hurry, scurrying hither and thither along the dockside. Many were wearing unusual and colourful clothing, some carrying huge burdens or baskets balanced on their heads, others waving their arms about and shouting or singing in strange, rapid, unfamiliar tongues.

'We're here, Eleanor!' announced Harriet. 'Now you shall see how we Burfords make our way in the world.'

The carriage had drawn up alongside an impressive building bearing highly polished brass plaques engraved with the names of companies accommodated within, and Eleanor felt an unexpected surge of pride when she spotted the gleaming 'Swann Burford Line' plate.

The Swann Burford office was midway along the third floor landing. Ledgers, bundles of charter documents, cargo manifests, bills of lading, notes and letters were neatly filed along shelves lining the walls, and three clerks ranging in years from youth to middle age were seated at a long counter, heads bent to their labours and pens scratching across coarse paper. Harriet entered without knocking, and the chief clerk instantly rose from his high desk to greet her.

'Good day to you, ma'am!' he exclaimed warmly. 'You're well, I hope?'

'Very well indeed, Mr Howells,' said Harriet with a smile, taking his hand. 'And yourself and Mrs Howells? And your new great-grandchild?'

'Hale and hearty, one and all.'

'Splendid!' Harriet turned, drew Eleanor forward, and made the introductions. 'Mr Howells has been with us since my father's name was engraved upon that panelled door, Eleanor. Without his loyalty and hard work, Swann Burford would not be the distinguished shipper it is today.'

Eleanor responded politely, and Joseph Howells ushered them towards the panelled door, which now bore her brother-in-law Malcolm Burford's name, and showed them into the inner office. 'Mr Malcolm is presently engaged at the Custom House, ma'am,' he explained. 'We expect his return before the hour. Meanwhile, might I arrange some tea?'

'Tea would be lovely,' Harriet said with a nod. Unbuttoning her gloves, she crossed the office to her grandson's cluttered mahogany desk. Removing her hat and setting it beside her gloves, she sat behind the desk and ran a keen eye across the pages of meticulous copperplate.

'Grandma!' cried Eleanor. 'Quick! Come and see!' The girl had opened one of the square windows overlooking the quayside, and was reaching out across the stone ledge. 'The ships' masts are so long, they reach right across the road!' she exclaimed in astonishment. 'Look, if I leaned just a bit further, I could touch them!'

'And probably fall out,' Harriet remarked drily, looking down to the congested dock road far below. Adjacent to it, ships of all sizes and flying many colours were crammed along the quay, loading and discharging cargo, taking on provisions, crews and emigrants; making ready to sail. 'The pointed timbers sticking out from the fronts of the ships are jib-booms, Eleanor. Masts are tall uprights for supporting sails. Schooners have at least two masts — one at the back, and one at the front,' she explained, adding proudly, 'The Swann Burford Line has three schooners, each of them well-found and Liverpool-built.'

Eleanor gazed at Harriet. 'How do you know so much about ships, Grandma?'

'I'm my father's daughter, Eleanor. I love the sea and ships every bit as much as he did. My fondest childhood memories are of voyages with him and Mother. I'd always be at Papa's side, asking endless questions about winds and tides, the stars and sun and navigation.' Harriet laughed, moving from the window towards three framed family portraits and indicating an oil painting of a white-haired gentleman with magnificent side-whiskers and the bluest eyes Eleanor had ever seen. 'That's my papa — Captain Cedric Swann. He founded the Swann Line, as it was in its early days.'

'He looks kind.' Eleanor considered the weather-beaten features of the seaman standing proudly upon the deck of his ship. The next picture showed him in this very office, with a slightly younger man at his side. 'Who's he?'

'Sydney Burford — my husband,' replied Harriet, smiling at the inquisitive girl beside her. 'Papa hadn't any sons, so in time he took Sydney as his partner. He had never been to sea in his life, but he was an astute man of business, and the Swann Burford Line prospered. This portrait was painted to mark their partnership.'

'And you married Sydney?'

'Yes, I did.'

Harriet moved along to the final painting. Portly and greying at the temples, Burford was portrayed seated at the mahogany desk, a small boy standing solemnly at his side. 'That's David, our son,' Harriet said, her fingertips touching the edge of the heavy frame. 'Sydney was much older than me. Soon after this portrait was painted, I was widowed and duly lost our second child, whom I was carrying.

My father had passed away the previous year, and Davy was a little boy, so Swann Burford became my responsibility. Joseph Howells and I managed the family firm together until David grew up. Later, we had to manage it again. For Peter and Malcolm, you see.'

Eleanor nodded, understanding. Her sister Madge had already told her that some twenty years ago, David Burford and his wife had left their children with Harriet at Withencroft before travelling to Liverpool. They'd been caught there when fever struck the town. Both perished, and Harriet had raised her two young grandsons in Pedlars Down.

'I always longed for a daughter — and later, a granddaughter.' Harriet's soft, unexpected words broke into Eleanor's thoughts. 'I wasn't blessed with either — until you came to Withencroft, my dear.'

Eleanor raised her eyes to the elderly woman, her bonny face solemn as she shyly slipped her small hand into

Harriet's. 'I've never had a granny, ever.'

'I — I'd say you and I are a fine match, then, wouldn't you?' murmured Harriet, gently squeezing the little hand within her own.

'Whatever can be keeping Joseph with our tea?'

* * *

'Those caraway bracks smell wonderful!' exclaimed Agnes, watching Rachel carefully withdrawing a half-dozen golden brown, heavily fruited loaves from the big oven and deftly sliding in two batches of spiced Advent biscuits. The friends had been busy with Christmas baking since first light. The old kitchen was warm and brightly lit, heady with the fragrance of nutmeg, cinnamon, cloves, apples, oranges, lemons, mulled elderberry cordial and ginger.

Without, it was bitterly cold with a fierce north-westerly wind. Sleety

November rain was driving against the latticed windows of the kitchen and slithering down the tall, narrow chimney to spit and hiss upon the crackling pine logs heaped and glowing in the huge stone fireplace.

'Is one of the bracks for Mr Cumstock?' went on Agnes, pink-cheeked from the warmth of the kitchen and the effort of grinding shining crystals from the hard slab of sugar. 'I recall you once saying caraway brack was his favourite.'

Rachel nodded, disappearing into the cool pantry and emerging with pots of preserved cherries and apricots for the Christmas buns. 'I always bake two for Earnest — one for eating now, and the other to keep and take with him when he travels down to the Midlands next month to spend Christmas with his daughter.'

'Speaking of Christmas arrangements,' said the younger woman a shade awkwardly when Rachel joined her at the huge oblong table and began sifting flour into a great earthenware bowl, 'Mother is getting up our usual festive party for a concert and, of course, you and Edward are invited. But I — well, I . . . ' Agnes's voice trailed off and her face reddened with more than the heat of the kitchen. 'I know you haven't had any word from Hugh yet — although I'm absolutely certain all will be well and his letter is merely delayed by weather or some such . . . But what I mean to say is — '

'I understand, Agnes,' interrupted Rachel softly, reaching across the table to place a floury hand on her friend's arm. 'And thank you for your thoughtfulness.' She turned sad eyes to the small-paned windows. The sleety rain was drier and thicker now, gathering up in greyish drifts against the lead-lights and ledges. 'Truth to tell, as Christmas approaches, I find myself dwelling more and more upon last year, when Hugh and I . . . Oh, Agnes, I feel such a fool being weepy,' she confided shakily, roughly brushing her cheek with the back of her hand. 'It isn't like me. And I'm scarce a lovelorn young girl, when all's said and done. But the very coming of the season stirs too many memories. A twelvemonth ago, Christmastide was filled with great joy and — and hope. It was the happiest of times. But this year without him . . . without even any word of him . . . there is only emptiness.'

★ ★ ★

They worked on until afternoon closed into dusk before wrapping up in bonnets, mufflers, mittens, capes and boots. Then, with heads bowed into the sleet and wind, they started down into the village. Agnes was going straight home, but Rachel took a basket of baking into the parsonage for Reverend Greenhalgh and then crossed the green to Meadow Well. It was dark by now, and the pupils long gone, so the only light showing at the schoolhouse was from Mr Cumstock's parlour window.

The schoolmaster had a kettle heating over the fire, and while he made tea, Rachel unpacked the basket. As well as the caraway bracks, she'd brought a hotpot topped with browned potato slices, freshly baked bread, a dish of butter churned that morning, and the first taste of this year's tangy festive cheese with its layer of sage and onion through the middle. They drank their tea and spoke a little of the school, though Rachel was keenly aware of the weariness in Mr Cumstock's kindly eyes and soon bade him a good night, leaving the elderly man to his supper and fireside.

The wind had dropped, the sleet ceased. The night was bitterly cold with a clear sky but barely a sliver of moon to light her way. Drawing the muffler closer about her neck, Rachel quickened her pace. She'd be glad to be home.

'Miss! Miss Warmsley!' The pot lad dashed from the yard of Millers Inn, a letter in his hand. 'T'master spotted you and said I was to go after you. You got post, miss!'

Fumbling in her purse for a coin for the boy and mumbling her thanks, Rachel clutched the letter in both hands. She scarce received them. It could only be from Hugh — or, worse, news of Hugh, or the ship he had sailed upon. Her heart froze with dread. What if . . .

It was too dark to make out the writing. She couldn't see if it was Hugh's own hand. And she had to know! Turning about, she sped across the green to St. Cuthbert's. The instant she pushed open the heavy west door and stepped within, flickering candle-light spilled upon Hugh Armstrong's distinctive handwriting. Weak at the knees and with tears of relief and gratitude springing to her eyes, Rachel at once whispered a prayer of thanks.

With steps that weren't quite steady, she started through the nave, and only then realised she was not alone. Partially concealed within deep wells of shadows beneath the arch, Harriet Burford was kneeling before the Burford memorial window, placing what Rachel assumed were the very last blooms of the year from Withencroft's sheltered flower gardens. There was the scent of a herb, too. Rosemary, that was it. Of course. Rosemary for remembrance.

'My apologies for disturbing you, Mrs Burford,' murmured Rachel, pausing where she stood. 'I didn't see you when I entered.'

'You haven't disturbed me, Rachel,' replied Harriet, rising to quit the church. The two women's eyes met briefly. 'Good evening to you.'

'And to you, Mrs Burford.'

In the candlelit quiet of the church, the scent of winter flowers and the pungent fragrance of rosemary filled the air. Rachel was alone with her prayers, her memories and her letter.

Hugh was safe. He was missing her, he was thinking of her, and he had kept his promise to write to her.

Eleanor decided Mosley's in Bold Street must be the grandest shop in the whole world. The haberdashery had a huge window at each side of the wide arched doorway, and the moment she and Harriet went inside, Mr Mosley himself hurried forward to welcome them. Eleanor was fast becoming accustomed to the deference folk paid to her grandmother, and to the Burford name.

Leaving Harriet and the haberdasher discussing flannel, she wandered further into the shop. Everywhere, such wonderful colours! Silks and satins shimmering like jewels in the clear light shed from fluted crystal oil lamps; shelves reaching from floor to ceiling, laden with bolts of muslins, damasks, velvets, brocades, cotton, linen, flannels and lawn. Upon long polished counters were displays of ribbons, lace, pins, needles, hoops, hooks, beads and great dishes of buttons. Entranced by the contents of one particular dish, Eleanor leaned across the counter, her head bowed to one side so she might get a closer look. It was just like magic! The fancy cut-glass buttons were glittering up at her, sparkling like lots and lots of tiny rainbows.

'What's caught your eye?' Harriet's voice startled her. She hadn't noticed Grandma joining her at the counter. 'Ah! The buttons! They *are* pretty, aren't they?'

'I've never seen buttons like those before!'

'Nor have I,' Harriet said with a smile. She continued, 'Mr Mosley is bringing some special flannels for us to look at. Now we know for certain that Marjorey is expecting, we can begin sewing for the baby's arrival next year.'

'It's funny to think I'll be an aunt,' remarked Eleanor, turning away from the buttons. 'And little Felix will be an uncle.'

'What about me? I will become a great-grandmama!' laughed Harriet.

'Ah, here comes Mr Mosley with the flannels. After we've chosen those, we'll need a selection of wools and ribbons. We'll be knitting and crocheting for the baby, as well as sewing.'

Eleanor looked doubtful. 'I'm better at drawing and painting than sewing and knitting, Grandma.'

'Yes, I've noticed that, my dear,' agreed Harriet amiably, patting the girl's shoulder. 'Never mind; with practice you'll improve in no time. And after we've our purchases for Marjorey and the baby, you must choose some pretty dress material to match those sparkly buttons you've taken such a fancy to!'

* * *

After the haberdashery, they made for the waterfront and the offices of the Swann Burford Line. 'Is that our ship?' asked Eleanor, standing next to her grandmother at the window and pointing down to the noisy, teeming quayside. 'Is that the one Peter's sailing away on?'

'Yes, that's the *Providence.*' Harriet was watching her eldest grandson and his crew making ready the schooner to sail with the tide. 'She's bound for the Indies. Did you find her route on your globe at home?'

Eleanor nodded. 'It's ever such a long way, isn't it?'

'It is indeed, and in these dangerous times . . . ' She left the sentence, and her unquiet thoughts, unspoken. Looking down at the little girl beside her, she smiled. 'This is our last trip into town before Christmas, so we must ensure we don't forget anything.

'Why don't you sit at Malcolm's desk and make a shopping list?' Clambering into the heavy carved chair, Eleanor took a sheet of paper bearing the Swann Burford name, dipped a pen into the brass and crystal inkwell, and glanced around to Harriet. 'I'm ready.'

'Our first port of call will be Poole

Lane,' said Harriet, still at the window with her gaze and attention focused upon the quayside and the *Providence's* preparations to sail. 'Since my father founded Swann Burford, it's been our custom to give Christmas boxes to every employee here at the office; cigars and chocolates to Mr Howell and Mrs Howell, and to our shipmasters and their wives. While I'm at the tobacconist's, you can walk further down Poole Lane to Kinvig's and choose chocolates for the ladies,' she went on methodically. 'I promised Reverend Greenhalgh I'd collect some books he's ordered from the stationer's, so add that to your list, too.'

Eleanor nodded, her pen scratching busily on the thick paper.

'While we're in Poole Lane,' concluded Harriet, 'we want seasonal gifts for the Whiteheads, Mr Cumstock, Reverend Greenhalgh and our other friends and neighbours in Pedlars Down.'

Eleanor paused in her writing. 'Will

we give anything to the Warmsleys?' she asked in a low voice, wondering if the question would vex her grandmother. But instead, it seemed to Eleanor that Harriet sounded rather sad when she replied.

'Many years ago, our families were close, and we did share our Christmases. But no, I'm afraid not, my dear. Those days of our families being neighbourly are long past.' She paused a moment, going on more cheerily, 'Before we set off on our shopping spree, you'd best have this!' She reached into her commodious bag to withdraw a little claret velvet drawstring purse that jingled when she placed it in Eleanor's small hands.

The purse felt heavy, and when Eleanor pulled open the strings and peeped inside, it was filled with shiny silver shillings. 'I've never had money before, Grandma!' she gasped, raising astonished eyes to Harriet.

'Then it's high time you did. Having money is a great responsibility, so think carefully about how you wish to use it.'

'Can I spend it on anything? Anything at all?'

'It's yours, Eleanor, and up to you to decide how you spend it.'

Harriet's attention had never strayed far from the proceedings down on the quayside, and now she started from the window. 'The *Providence* is about to sail. Come along, we'll go down and see her off.'

'Do you always watch our ships sail away, Grandma?' asked Eleanor when they'd said their goodbyes to Captain Peter and were standing on the quayside watching him stride aboard the schooner and take his place on deck.

'I do. I always like to keep in my memory our ships sailing out into the open sea.'

'Peter won't be home for Christmas, will he?'

'Nor will many a sailor, Eleanor,' replied Harriet soberly. 'Seafaring is a lonely life, for the men who sail and for their families left ashore — especially at Christmastide.'

Eleanor felt her grandmother's arm slip about her shoulders, and together they stood on the quayside, watching the *Providence* sail from their sight.

★　★　★

Poole Lane was a narrow, crooked thoroughfare in the oldest part of the town. Lined with quality shops, on this winter's morning shortly before Christmas it was especially busy and crowded with ladies and gentlemen browsing the crescent of brightly lit windows offering all manner of exquisite goods.

Eleanor felt rather grand choosing from the array of chocolates, sweets and candies in Kinvig's, and very grown up giving instructions for their delivery to the chocolatier exactly as she'd observed her grandmother doing. She emerged from the shop with a bag of barley sugar twists for her young brother, Felix, who in a few days would be coming home from school for the holidays. The rest of the shillings in the little velvet purse jingled in her pocket. Now that she had lots of money, she could buy a really special present — but what?

Swept up amongst the crush of shoppers, Eleanor searched window after window along the dog-leg lane, and was almost at the furthest end before she spotted the very thing. Yes, that was it! Pushing open the genteel establishment's ornately carved door and setting the brass bell above it jangling, Eleanor stepped inside to make her purchase.

* * *

Laden with boxes, curiously shaped packages and parcels, and securely wrapped and corded bolts of cloth and skeins of wool, Eleanor and Harriet quit their rooms at the Rutherford Hotel and, travelling at a sedate pace, reached Pedlars Down early in the afternoon.

'I'll take these books to Reverend Greenhalgh,' Harriet was saying when the carriage drew alongside the parsonage. 'I must have a word with him upon parish affairs, too. Are you coming with me, Eleanor?'

'Hmm?' Her sharp eyes had spotted a familiar figure and his dog talking to Cully, the blacksmith's lad. She turned from the window to her grandmother. 'I'd rather walk about a bit and stretch my legs, Grandma.'

'Good idea. We've been seated far too long,' responded Harriet, alighting stiffly from the carriage. 'Don't wander too far though — I'm well aware how easily you lose track of time!'

No sooner had Harriet entered the parsonage than Eleanor was out of the carriage and scurrying across the green towards the forge. Jonas hadn't yet seen her, and she was about to give their owl-hoot signal to attract his attention when Rupert's nose twitched, his brown silky head went up, and with ears whirling he raced from Jonas's side and made a beeline for Eleanor. Jonas instantly followed suit but veered off, ducking from sight around the corner of Millers Inn. A moment later, Eleanor and Rupert joined him there.

'What luck seeing you as soon as we got back!' she exclaimed, kneeling and hugging Rupert but raising her happy face to Jonas. 'Me and Grandma — Grandma and I, I mean — have been in Liverpool — ' She broke off, puzzled. 'Why are you looking at me like that?'

Jonas shrugged awkwardly, stuffing his hands deep into the pockets of his coarse homespun winter coat. It had been Edward's when he was a boy. 'I dunno,' he mumbled, shuffling his boots and from beneath lowered eyes taking in Eleanor's smartly tailored cherry-red coat and skirt, velvet-trimmed bonnet and shiny little boots. 'You're all done up. Like a proper lady.'

'Oh.' Eleanor glanced absently at her outfit. 'This is new. It's for winter travelling. Grandma had it made for me. We mightn't see each other again

106

before Christmas, Jonas,' she went on, beaming and offering him a small parcel. 'So this is for you — merry Christmas!'

Crestfallen, Jonas stared down at the package neatly wrapped in thick brown paper and tied with string. He made no attempt to take it from her. 'What is it?'

'Open it and find out!' She laughed, pushing the parcel into his hands.

Slowly, without once meeting Eleanor's eyes, Jonas did as he was bidden. 'Gloves,' he whispered, colour flushing to his smooth cheeks. 'I never had gloves before.'

'They're to keep your hands warm.'

'I know what gloves are for!' he retorted roughly.

'Don't you like them?' murmured Eleanor, disappointed. 'I — I went in the shop and got them all by myself.'

'Aye, 'course I like 'em,' he returned hurriedly, pulling himself together and smiling down into her sad, upturned little face. 'They're a grand present! It's just . . . I haven't got a present for *you*.

'I don't have any brass, Lenny — I *never* have any brass of me own — I can't buy owt for you!'

'Oh, that doesn't matter at all!' exclaimed Eleanor, happy again and stooping once more to wrap her arms about the pup sitting beside them. 'I've always longed for a dog, and you let me share Rupert. He's the very best gift you could ever give me, Jonas.'

Then she was gone, dashing off across the green towards the Burford carriage. She half-turned, waving to him. Jonas returned Eleanor's goodbye wave, forlornly watching her go and clutching the expensive gloves in his rough hands.

* * *

Late on Christmas Eve, Harriet led her family and household along the sandy moon-washed paths from Withencroft toward St. Cuthbert's. While she walked, with Eleanor and little Felix at her side, her thoughts were many miles from Pedlars Down, with Captain Peter and his crew aboard the *Providence*, bound for the Indies and so very, very far from home this Christmastide.

'Grandma, look at our shadows!' cried Felix as they rounded the broad curve between berry-laden hedgerows; and suddenly tall, dark figures were walking before them. 'There are *two* of each of us — and the others are coming to church with us!'

'My shadow is waving to yours, Felix,' laughed Eleanor, glancing past Harriet to her young brother. 'See?'

'And mine is waving back!'

Presently the village came into sight, with the illuminated stained-glass windows of St. Cuthbert's glowing in the distance, its medieval bell pealing. From all directions, friends and neighbours were coming together, making their way inside.

More candles than usual were burning within, their golden light flickering warmly on the sandstone walls and pillars. Agnes Whitehead was already settled at the organ, the fiddlers were tuning up, and the young lad with the flute was trying to catch the eye of a pretty girl sitting close by.

The Burfords took their places, and Harriet gently squeezed the hands of Eleanor and Felix, seated at either side of her. 'This is our very first Christmas together,' she whispered with a smile. 'May we share many more!'

'The church looks so beautiful,' murmured Eleanor in wonder. 'I'd love to paint it all!'

'Then you must,' encouraged Harriet, admiring the festive swaths of scarlet-berried holly, glossy and variegated ivies, fragrant Scots pine and pale green mistletoe adorning window ledges, pulpit, end pews and arches. This was Rachel Warmsley's handiwork, Harriet knew. The strong, intelligent young woman had inherited her mother's delicate touch for arranging flowers and evergreens.

Harriet's thoughts strayed across the

aisle to the Warmsleys gathered in their family pew, and her gaze rested upon Rachel. She was smiling and nodding, talking quietly with her father and brothers. The notes of the first carol were drifting up to the vaulted roof and Harriet rose to her feet with a sigh. If life had turned out differently, Rachel Warmsley might have been *her* daughter . . .

4

Winter snows were smothering distant hills. The only greenery in Boyo's Wood was moss and the ivies carpeting the cold earth and cleaving to gnarled, skeletal old trees.

'I'd love to come, Jonas!' Eleanor frowned, flopping down beside him on the fallen lightning bole. 'But I can't — it's too risky.'

'Look, do you want to see Clover and her foal or not?' he demanded irritably.

'Of course I do!' she exclaimed earnestly. 'You know I do! I've never seen a new-born foal. It's just, well . . . I don't want us to get caught, that's all.'

'What you mean is,' he went on crossly, 'you don't want old Granny Burford finding out we're pals.'

'You don't want your pa to find out,' countered Eleanor, adding briskly,

'Anyhow, it isn't Grandma who's going to see us sneaking into Clover's stable, is it? It'll be your sister, or worse yet, your pa. You're the one who told me he's fierce against Burfords, remember!'

'Aye, that's true enough,' Jonas had to admit, but he pressed on regardless. 'Pa won't be anywhere near the house, though. He and Edward are miles away, working up at Blea. And I heard Rachel saying she's turning the beds or summat this morning, so she'll be busy upstairs and won't see us nipping in and out of the yard. It'll be all right, Lenny, I promise!' he concluded, getting to his feet and stretching his hand toward her. 'Are you coming or not?'

They approached the manor house cautiously, keeping to the cover of holly bushes and broad tree trunks as they drew near. Everywhere did appear still and quiet, but Eleanor felt uneasy just the same. She elbowed Jonas in the ribs, whispering, 'Go and make sure nobody's about — I'll wait here with Rupert.'

She watched him sauntering down toward the house, passing Billy grazing under leafless trees, turning around the old coach-house corner and briefly disappearing into the cobbled stable-yard. Then Jonas was back, signalling for her to come quickly. Jamming her wide-brimmed hat more firmly down over her curls and hitching up her hand-me-down breeches, Eleanor ran to join him.

'We're safe as houses!' he grinned triumphantly. 'The kindling wagon's out front of the stables, so you can nip round behind it and straight inside — I've opened up the doors.'

Clover and her foal were settled in deep wheat-and-oat straw. 'Wish I'd brought something for her and her baby,' murmured Eleanor, kneeling beside them. 'We've plenty of apples at home.'

'The foal only drinks milk, and you've got to watch giving Clover apples,' remarked Jonas. 'They sometime give her the grip, but I'll fetch a carrot from the kitchen. She can't have many, but a carrot now and again is all right.'

He was coming out of the kitchen with a carrot and a couple of currant buns he'd found in the pantry when one of the upstairs casements flew open and Rachel leaned out, looking hot and dusty with a polishing rag in one hand and a dish of beeswax in the other. 'Jonas!' she called sharply. 'Why are you still here? That kindling wagon won't take itself down to the village!'

He spun around, glaring up at her. 'I'm taking it later.'

'You'll take it now!' she returned severely. 'There'll likely be needy folk in the parish waiting on that firewood. Shape yourself, Jonas — don't stand there dawdling! Hitch up Billy and be on your way. And after you've delivered the kindling, I don't want you idling about the village, either — come straight home!' She withdrew from the window, and the casement closed firmly.

Mutinously, Jonas did as he was bidden, making much of fetching Billy and hitching the sturdy black horse up to the heavily-laden wagon stacked with dead wood gathered from the plantation and chopped into kindling. Then, with a furtive glance to check Rachel wasn't still there watching him, he dived into Clover's stable and looked around for Eleanor. 'Where *are* you?' he hissed.

'Here,' she returned, scrambling to her feet and emerging from an empty stall. 'I hid in case your sister came down.'

'I'll leave the stable door open,' said Jonas, glowering up at the manor house windows, 'and bring around the kindling wagon. When I stop and come to shut the door, you sneak out and climb into the wagon. Lie low till I tell you. Have you got that?'

She nodded, shaking straw from her hair and grabbing her hat. 'Got it!'

Once she was safely within the wagon-bed, Jonas threw an old sack across her until they were away from the manor house, then she scrambled up onto the seat beside him.

'I've had my fill of this,' fumed Jonas, glancing sidelong at his companion who, in her breeches, hat and homespun coat, looked just like one of the village lads. 'I don't care what anybody says, I'm going to get a job and be done with it!'

'You said you'd never work for Fred Leach!'

'Nor will I,' retorted Jonas, adding stubbornly, 'There's other folk to work for besides him.'

'Who?' persisted Eleanor. 'Where else is there?'

'I dunno, exactly,' he conceded. Then a notion hit him full-square. 'In town, Lenny! Aye, that's it! There's bound to be hundreds of jobs going in town!'

'I suppose,' she considered, recalling trips into Liverpool with her grandmother. 'Yes, I've seen boys working with the horses at the hotel, and lots and lots of them down on the waterfront.'

But Jonas wasn't listening. His eyes were bright and excited, and when he turned to look down at Eleanor, a huge grin was spreading across his face. 'Armstrong's, Lenny! That's where Rachel's old sweetheart worked. And Pa's known Sam Armstrong since they were young. I'll borrow Edward's horse, go down town and get a job at Armstrong's,' vowed Jonas eagerly. 'I'll do it, Lenny, first chance I get. You just see if I don't!'

★ ★ ★

Jonas was forced to bide his time. Days turned into weeks, and it got harder and harder to toe the line, get on with his chores, go to school every day, keep out of scrapes and bite his tongue whenever Rachel scolded him, all the while making sure he didn't let slip a word about his plans.

The chance finally came when Pa and Edward were coppicing hazel over at Spinney and, it being market day,

Rachel was certain to be out from early morning. After breakfast, Jonas set off for school as usual, but holed up in Boyo's Wood until he reckoned the coast would be clear. Then he sped back home, dressed in his Sunday best clothes, saddled Edward's horse, and started for the Liverpool road.

Although Jonas had been into town before, with Pa and Edward on the wagon, this was the first time he'd gone there alone and on horseback. He'd no idea where Armstrong's was, and he needed to find somewhere safe to leave Edward's horse and have him rubbed down, fed and watered while he went looking. Jonas hadn't thought to bring any food with him, either, and he was hungry himself now. At least he'd had sense enough to scoop a handful of coins from Rachel's housekeeping tin. He'd repay the money when he got his first week's wages.

Jonas didn't have much luck asking folk for directions to the cotton merchant's until he spotted a pie-man selling his wares outside the flock works. He bought a pie, was told about a trustworthy livery down the next street, and given a convoluted set of directions that led him into the heart of the commercial quarter of town.

By and by, Jonas navigated the maze of tall soot-blackened buildings and entered the premises of Samuel and Henry Armstrong, Cotton Merchants. 'I'm here to see Mr Armstrong,' he said, stepping up to the clerk's desk. 'I want to work here.'

'Do you, now?' remarked the clerk, briefly raising his eyes from a ledger to look Jonas up and down before returning his attention to book-keeping. 'On your way, boy — Armstrong's has no place for the likes of you.'

Jonas didn't move a muscle. He stood his ground, glowering at the clerk's bent head, a flame of hot, quick anger uncurling inside him. He'd taken Edward's horse without asking; he'd helped himself from Rachel's house-keeping tin; he'd gone back on his word to her and to old Cumstock about school; he'd told Lenny he'd get a job at Armstrong's. He wasn't about to give up and go home with his tail between his legs because some uppity pen-pusher reckoned he wasn't good enough! He'd stay put till he saw Sam Armstrong — and if this clerk or anybody else didn't like it, they'd have to chuck him out!

'I'm Jonas Warmsley,' he announced defiantly, striving to curb his temper and be polite like Edward would. 'My pa — father — is Squire Ben Warmsley of Pedlars Down. He and Sam Armstrong are old friends.'

The clerk looked up again, pursing his lips and considering Jonas suspiciously. 'A friend of Mr Armstrong's, you say?'

'Aye. Squire Ben Warmsley,' repeated Jonas firmly, squaring his shoulders. 'The pair of 'em have known each other since they were lads.'

'Wait here.' The clerk scraped back his chair and crossed the floor, disappearing into an adjoining room only to emerge almost immediately. 'Mr Armstrong will see you, Master Warmsley.'

Striding past the clerk and into a high-ceilinged office, Jonas came face to face with Samuel Armstrong.

'My clerk tells me you're Ben Warmsley's boy,' he barked, appraising Jonas shrewdly. 'You've the look of him, right enough. You'll be his youngest, I take it?'

'Aye, sir.'

'Ben and I haven't run into each other much these recent years. How's your pa keeping?'

'Well enough, sir.'

'And he's sent you down here to see me?'

Jonas faltered and gave a quick shake of his head. 'It was my idea, sir.'

Sam Armstrong's keen eyes narrowed, his gaze boring into the boy standing before him. Jonas glanced away, squirming under the scrutiny.

'I daresay there's plenty of work to be done at Pedlars Down,' pondered Armstrong. 'In its way, it's a family concern exactly like this one. What does your pa say about you coming down here asking me for a job?'

Jonas cleared his throat, meeting the cotton merchant's eyes steadily. 'He dun't know owt about it, sir. Pa dun't know I'm here.'

Sam Armstrong leaned back in his upholstered chair, considering Jonas's earnest face, and nodded slowly. 'You'd best sit down, Master Warmsley, and tell me exactly what brings you to Armstrong's — and why I should contemplate taking you on.'

Jonas's confidence faltered. He knew that whatever he said to Armstrong would make or break him. His whole life was in this man's hands. Everything Jonas wanted was his for the winning — or the losing.

'I want summat of me own, sir,' he blurted suddenly. 'I've got nowt that's not handed out to me by Pa or my brother or Rachel — and I've had enough of it. I want to get away from the village, and — and — make summat of myself,' Jonas went on rapidly. 'That's why I come here, sir. I'm sick of running errands and doing chores and being at everybody's beck and call! I want a proper job, where I earn a man's wage and can go where I like and see who I like and don't have to answer to nobody. Give me a chance to prove myself,' he implored urgently. 'I swear I'll work hard — I'll not let you down!'

Sam Armstrong didn't speak; just sat across the desk, his unblinking gaze fixed upon Jonas's face. The boy shifted uncomfortably. 'You remind me of myself when I was young,' mused the cotton merchant at length. 'I well recall the gnawing ambition that gave me no rest, day nor night. Aye, I'll give you your chance, Jonas Warmsley,' he concluded, adding, 'But take heed — I don't tolerate shirkers. You prove yourself worthy of your position here, or you'll be out of that door so fast your head will spin!'

* * *

'Taking Edward's horse and going off goodness knows where,' Rachel was complaining that evening while she cleared the supper table. 'It's getting late, Pa. Where is he? And what's he up to? Nothing good, I'll be bound!'

'Oh, don't worritt the lad so much,' remarked Ben, settling himself in the chimney corner and lighting his clay pipe. 'Happen there's a lass somewhere he's sweet on and he's trying to impress her. He'll come home when he's ready. Jonas is nearly a man grown,' he finished, drawing contentedly on the strong tobacco. 'You can't go on mollying him like he's still a bairn, y'know.'

'Pa!' She spun around from the table in exasperation. 'Jonas has to — ' Rachel broke off as Rupert leapt up from the hearth, where he'd been curled up and sleeping, and dashed to the kitchen door, scraping at it with both front paws until it creaked open and Jonas stepped inside. His face was flushed, his eyes unusually bright, and

Rachel's first suspicion was that he'd been ale-drinking with Cully or one of the other older village lads.

Before she could draw breath to admonish her rebellious younger brother, Jonas marched right into the kitchen, glancing at her briefly before turning to their father. 'Pa, I'm done with school,' he announced proudly. 'I've been to town and got a position at Armstrong's. Mr Armstrong said to give you his regards. I'm starting work come Monday. I'm sorry I took your housekeeping money, Rachel,' went on Jonas calmly, looking around at her. 'I'll pay it back from my first wages.'

'We can discuss your taking what doesn't belong to you later,' snapped Rachel. 'As for your starting work on Monday — the only place you're going is to school!'

'Steady on, now, Rachel,' countered Ben mildly. 'The lad's had the gumption to go into town and get himself a job with a fine firm like Armstrong's. Sam Armstrong isn't a man who's easily impressed, so you've done well there.' He beamed at Jonas. 'I'm right proud of you, son!'

'But Pa — '

'I've said my piece, Rachel,' cut in Ben firmly. 'There's an end to it. Fetch some supper for your brother. Jonas, you come and tell me all about it. How's old Sam doing?'

Fuming with frustration, Rachel said nothing and merely busied herself preparing Jonas's meal. She had no choice but accept her father's decision, nor could she question it. Nevertheless, she was convinced he was dreadfully mistaken. For all Pa's saying Jonas was nearly a man grown, she was fearful for her headstrong brother's safekeeping. Liverpool was a huge, crowded, unruly port — and for a young boy alone, surely a town fraught with danger and temptations.

* * *

'Whatever am I going to do now you won't be here?' Eleanor asked forlornly, looking up into Jonas's ruddy, eager face. They'd met up in Boyo's Wood. It was very early on a dark, frosty morning — the day he was starting work at Armstrong's. 'I'll have nobody to play with or talk to,' she murmured, stuffing cold hands into the pockets of her breeches. 'Felix has gone back to school, and Madge is always resting or getting ready for the baby.'

'I had to do it, Lenny,' responded Jonas. 'A man has to make his own way in this world.'

'You're not a man!' she protested shakily. 'You're only fourteen!'

'I'm man enough to get a proper job at Armstrong's instead of being ordered about like a bairn here in Pedlars Down and never having a penny piece in my pocket!' he argued vehemently, adding more gently, 'Couldn't stand it anymore, Lenny. I were trapped in this village. I had to get away and do summat on my own bat. Try to understand, will you?'

Eleanor bowed her head, nodding

sadly, her eyes swimming with tears she was determined not to shed.

'Ay, come on! Don't cry, little lass,' he mumbled shyly, awkwardly patting Eleanor's shoulder. 'I need you to do summat. Will you look after Rupert for me? After me, he loves you best. I have to go now, Lenny, but I'll find some way of seeing you after I get home tonight.'

Eleanor stood watching him walk away, his boots crunching in the thick frost. She watched till he turned through Boyo's Wood and was gone. Wandering back beneath the bare winter trees, she sank onto the lightning bole and put her arm around Rupert's rough neck. Tears started rolling down Eleanor's bonny cheeks, and the big pup gazed up at her with huge, sad amber eyes.

'Oh, Rupert,' she whispered, hugging him tight. 'I miss Jonas a lot already. Nothing's ever going to be the same, is it?'

* * *

Five years later . . .

The whole village was busy preparing for the harvest celebrations. Since she'd arrived in Pedlars Down, harvest thanksgiving had been one of Eleanor's favourite occasions. This year, however, she was especially looking forward to the festivities because her grandmother had decided that now Eleanor was a young lady, she might stay for the dancing rather than being taken home directly after the harvest supper was cleared.

'Miss Burford!'

Ernest Cumstock put his head around the door of the tithe barn, looking within to where Eleanor was unpacking a huge tea-chest of sturdy plates, bowls and mugs.

'The rest of the boards and trestles have arrived,' he went on cheerfully. 'Will it disturb you if we start setting them up?'

'Not at all, Mr Cumstock.' She beamed, indicating the jumble of boxes, baskets, jars, chests and stacks of

130

crockery heaped about her. 'Once they're up, I can begin organising everything.'

A moment later the elderly schoolmaster came back into the barn, hefting one end of a large, somewhat battered pine board. At the other end was a dark-eyed man Eleanor didn't recognise. When the board was placed securely upon two stout trestles, Mr Cumstock made the introductions.

'This is Thadius Sawyer from Connecticut in New England,' he said, glancing to the young man standing beside him. 'He's painting St. Cuthbert's, Miss Burford, and offered to lend a hand with our harvest preparations.'

'It's extremely kind of you, Mr Sawyer,' responded Eleanor politely, indicating their cluttered surroundings with a graceful sweep of her hand. 'As you can see, we sorely need all the help we can get.'

'Glad to pitch in, ma'am,' Thadius Sawyer returned with an easy smile.

'Looks like it's going to be quite a night!'

'We hope so,' laughed Eleanor, brushing a stray chestnut curl from her forehead and delving into a hamper of bunting. 'We certainly hope so!'

The two men had no sooner quit the tithe barn than Eleanor sensed someone else entering, and was caught about her waist by strong arms.

'I thought old Cumstock and that stranger would never go!' Jonas's low voice was close against Eleanor's ear, his lips lightly brushing her cheek before she whirled around, looping her arms about his neck and raising her face to his, her eyes sparkling.

'Whatever are *you* doing here?' she exclaimed, surprised and immeasurably happy to see him. 'And why are you still wearing your going-to-business clothes?'

'I'm just come from Armstrong's, that's why. Sam Armstrong told me I could knock off early today.' He grinned. 'Seeing as how it isn't every day a man gets promoted!'

'Promoted?' she gasped. 'Congratulations! Tell me every last detail!'

'One of the senior clerks has taken up a commission in his father's old regiment or some such, so Mr Armstrong's promoted me to his position,' he explained proudly. 'It's a big step-up, y'know, Lenny. I'll be getting a lot more money now, and this is only the start! I'll go far at Armstrong's. There's fortunes to be made in cotton.'

'It's wonderful news, Jonas — and richly deserved!' she said warmly. 'You've worked hard these five years. I'm certain Mr Armstrong could not manage without you now.'

'Sam Armstrong's taught me more about the cotton trade than most men ever know. He says I remind him of himself when he was young. And we do see eye to eye about business, him and me,' went on Jonas, gazing down into her eyes and stroking the softness of her hair. 'I've not seen you for days, Lenny. What've you been doing?'

'Baking,' she laughed, spinning from

his embrace and returning to her duties. 'Tarts, pies, cakes, biscuits, buns, turnovers — you name it, we Withencroft women have baked it for tonight's festivities.'

He grimaced. 'All anybody talks about is this blasted harvest social!'

'I think it's a lovely tradition,' she countered blithely, her pretty face rosy as she worked. 'The whole village celebrating bringing in the harvest.'

Jonas frowned. 'I was reckoning on you and me celebrating my promotion tonight; maybe start making some plans for the future.' Catching both Eleanor's busy hands, he held them fast, drawing her closer. 'Everyone will be down here at the social. For once, we can meet without sneaking around.' He broke off, his breathing ragged at her nearness. 'I just want to *be* with you, Lenny!'

Wriggling free, Eleanor looked up at him incredulously. 'What about the harvest supper and the dancing?'

'I'm not bothered about that,' he snorted derisively.

'*I* am,' she returned stoutly, bustling past him to the cart and bringing in yet another basket. 'I've been looking forward to this evening for weeks!'

'You're surely never coming?' he demanded in disbelief.

'Of course I'm coming.' She didn't pause in unpacking the basket of Lancashire huffs. 'There'll be musicians and singers and dancing by lantern-light till long past midnight. It's going to be wonderful, Jonas! Aren't you looking forward to it, even a little?'

He stared at her as though she'd taken leave of her wits. 'What's the point?' he demanded. 'It's not like I can dance with you, is it?'

'I won't mind you dancing with other girls,' she replied lightly. 'Providing you don't enjoy it too much!'

Eleanor was smiling, but Jonas's face was darker than thunder. 'Don't you want us to be together?'

'Of course I do! Celebrating your promotion is a fine idea, but it can't be this evening,' she protested reasonably.

'Surely you must see that?'

He glowered down at her, his angry eyes sweeping her from head to toe. 'I'm not sure *what* I see anymore, Lenny!'

'Jonas!' she cried, alarmed and reaching out for him even as he turned on his heel away from her. 'Don't.'

It was too late. He stormed from the tithe barn without a backward glance.

* * *

Mellow afternoon sunlight was pouring through the open doors of St. Cuthbert's while Rachel, Walter Cruickshank and Reverend Greenhalgh made ready for the blessing of the harvest.

'My word, Mr Cruickshank,' Rachel said, stepping back to better admire the crusty golden-brown wheatsheaf at the heart of their traditional harvest display of fruits, vegetables and grain, 'you've outdone yourself. It's truly a wonder!'

'Ah, you say that every year, Miss Rachel,' countered the baker modestly, nonetheless looking pleased as he surveyed his handiwork. 'It's naught but flour, yeast, salt and water, thou knows.'

'And you say *that* every year.' She laughed, still marvelling at the enormous loaf of bread fashioned as a bundle of wheat, each of a hundred and more ears ripe on its stalk, and the whole sheaf bound around the middle with a twist of dough and baked to perfection in the Cruickshank family's ancient stone oven.

Leaving the baker putting finishing touches to the display, Rachel emerged from the quietude of the church into the noise and bustle without. As preparations for the evening's festivities gathered pace, you could scarce put a pin between folk darting back and forth across the village. As usual, Fred Leach was in the thick of it, yelling orders and curses to all and sundry, and adding to the frantic flurry was the dusty, travel-stained mail coach just arrived at Millers Inn and hastily disgorging its passengers, who had but a brief respite for refreshment before fresh horses were harnessed and the coach speeding on its route again.

Giving Fred Leach and his men a wide berth, Rachel was skirting the green when she noticed Ernest Cumstock a short distance from the coach. He had his back to her, head bowed and standing stock-still, oblivious to the commotion around him.

She hurried to his side. 'Ernest, are you quite well?'

The elderly schoolmaster started violently, turning toward her, and Rachel saw he was holding a letter with both hands; hands that were trembling.

'You've had bad news,' she murmured, for there could be no mistaking the shock and anguish in his eyes. 'Is it from your daughter, Ernest — is it from May?'

'It's Robert, her husband,' he murmured, roughly rubbing the back of his hand across his eyes. 'He's dead, Rachel — Robert's dead!'

138

Taking Mr Cumstock's arm, Rachel guided him towards the privacy of the schoolhouse. Once indoors, she sat him down at the fireside and set to making tea. Despite the warmth of the afternoon, Mr Cumstock was shivering, and Rachel fetched a counterpane from the adjoining bedroom and wrapped it about his hunched shoulders.

'Robert's been killed,' he said, offering her the letter. 'Accident at the foundry. He was like a son to me, Rachel.'

'I know he was,' she said sadly, scanning May's hastily scribbled lines. 'You must go to your family at once, Earnest. I'll make enquiries at the inn to find when the next coach bound for Birmingham leaves Liverpool.'

'I can't go,' he said wearily, shaking his head and staring down into the cup of strong sweet tea. 'The school . . . I can't simply up and leave the school.'

'You have no choice,' Rachel reasoned gently. 'May needs you. There'll be arrangements to be made. You can take those responsibilities from her shoulders. And your grandchildren — they're too young to understand what's happened. Your place is there, with them. Drink your tea, and take this little while to gather yourself,' she concluded quietly. 'I'm going over to the inn. I won't be long. When I get back, I'll pack some belongings and Edward will drive you into Liverpool.'

Finding out when the evening coach departed Liverpool for Birmingham was straightforward enough; locating her brother and the wagon not so much. After asking several people, Rachel discovered Edward had already returned home. Another arrangement for taking Ernest into town must be made, and quickly.

Hurrying back toward the schoolhouse — for she was loath to leave him too long alone — Rachel glanced up at the clock at St. Cuthbert's. If Ernest was to be aboard that coach and bound for his daughter's home this night, he'd need to be on his way to Liverpool within the half-hour.

She reached the schoolhouse as a man she'd recently seen about the village was coming out. 'You must be Rachel? Mr Cumstock's just told me about his son-in-law,' said Thadius Sawyer briskly, offering his hand and adding as an afterthought, 'I've been helping him with the harvest preparations, ma'am. Thadius Sawyer.'

She nodded, distractedly taking his hand and briefly explaining the situation. 'So you see, there's not a moment to be lost, Mr Sawyer. Will you stay with Ernest while I hire a vehicle and driver from the inn?'

'No need, ma'am. I'll gladly drive him into Liverpool. My horses and wagon are only a piece away. I'll fetch them directly and be out front here whenever Mr Cumstock is ready to go. I'm a stranger in Pedlars Down, and he's made me welcome; befriended me,' finished Thadius, already striding from the schoolhouse. 'It's the least I can do.'

Within the quarter-hour, both men

were aboard Sawyer's wagon, drawing away from the village toward the Liverpool road. Inevitably, word of Mr Cumstock's urgent departure swiftly spread, and some folk had gathered to offer condolences and see him off. They were dispersing now, and Rachel was about to do the same. She hadn't been aware of Fred Leach's sidling up alongside her; and when she turned for the schoolhouse, his burly frame blocked her path.

'Sad news, Miss Warmsley,' he breathed down at her, his mouth twisting into a sneer. 'Sad news indeed. Can't run a school with no teacher, can you now?'

★ ★ ★

Jonas intended putting as much distance as possible between himself and Pedlars Down that harvest night. He'd planned on heading into town, meeting friends at the Saracen's Head and playing cards all night long.

Right enough, he hadn't shown up with his family for the harvest supper, but nor had he ridden into Liverpool. Under cover of gathering darkness, he'd tethered Blaze beneath the sprawling chestnut trees and stolen close to the tithe barn. He saw Lenny arriving with old Granny Burford and the rest of the clan. He watched Captain Peter handing Lenny down from the carriage, her thin summer frock floating about her as she moved. Jonas's breath constricted in his chest. It was all he could do not to yell her name, race from his hiding place, grab her hand and — and — what?

Burning with frustration, Jonas felt beads of sweat prickling the back of his neck and ran a finger around the starched white collar of his shirt. He should've gone straight into Liverpool. Still and all, he couldn't tear himself away. The tithe barn doors were thrown open to the balmy night air, and he hunkered down. Hidden from sight. Watching.

The musicians struck up and dancers took to the floor. Lenny danced first with Captain Peter, next with Malcolm Burford; and then some cocky-looking redcoat officer who'd come with the Whiteheads' party took Lenny's hand and led her into the dance. She was gazing up at the lieutenant as they turned and swayed and dipped. He was holding her close. He had his arms about her. He put his mouth to her ear as he whispered something that made her blush and smile into his eyes . . .

Jonas could bear no more of it! Seething jealousy and the heat of his passion flared. Fists clenched, Jonas scrambled to his feet — then froze. Somebody was behind him.

'Leave it be, son.'

Jonas's every muscle was taut. He didn't turn around. 'How long have you been standing there, Pa?'

'Long enough,' Ben Warmsley answered evenly. 'To watch you — watching *her.*'

'What of it?' snapped Jonas, his gaze

144

not shifting from the tithe barn. 'Nowt wrong with watching the dancing, is there?'

'Happen not. But rush in there all riled up to thump that soldier boy, and you'll make a right fool of yourself,' remarked Ben, adding, 'Yon Miss Burford'll not thank 'ee for showing her up in front of the whole village, that's for certain.'

Jonas shrugged. 'Makes no never-mind to me. Why would it?'

'I'm not daft, lad. I were young myself once,' chided Ben, shaking his head. 'One look at that face of yours, and it's plain as day you're sweet on the girl.'

'I've a good job and brass of my own now,' Jonas rounded on his father. 'I shall wed Lenny one day, just as soon as we both come of age. Neither you nor old Granny Burford'll be able to stand in our way then!'

'That's true,' agreed Ben amiably. 'And Miss Eleanor's a fine girl. Bright as a button and sharp as a pin, from what I've heard. The kind of lass who'll turn many a young man's head. But no good can come of this fancy of yours, son! She's not right for you, and her family will never — '

'I want Lenny,' cut in Jonas. 'No family feud's going to keep us apart!'

'There's been bad blood between our families, right enough, but that's got nowt to do with it,' argued Ben. 'The Burfords — they're not our sort, lad. They've more brass than they know what to do with — and they're not short on airs and graces either. You go courting that girl, and mark my words, you'll come off worst. You'll be left standing. For when the time comes, she'll do what families like them always do — marry well and make a good match,' he concluded, adding, 'Why, the Burfords have likely got some rich and fancy gent already picked out for her.'

The fire and fight ebbed from Jonas. The treachery of his own doubts and insecurities suddenly crowded in. 'Lenny's the only one for me,' he mumbled stubbornly. 'Seeing her with that soldier; seeing her dancing with him like that . . . Ah, what's the point, Pa? You wouldn't understand.'

Ben drew breath to speak but bit his tongue. His eyes were troubled as he looked upon his youngest son. 'Come in to your family and friends,' he urged at length. 'There's plenty of other pretty lasses to dance with, y'know.'

Jonas shook his head, starting towards Blaze.

'Where are you going?'

'Town. I've a promotion to celebrate.'

Brooding, Jonas rode from Pedlars Down. Leaving Eleanor, the lantern-light, music and dancing of the harvest festivities far behind, he made for Liverpool and the many diversions at the Saracen's Head.

* * *

Comely Miss Eleanor Burford was very much the topic of gossip and speculation amongst those ladies who were seated around the tithe barn keeping time to the lively tunes, observing the dancing — and eyeing up the dancers.

'She's a pretty one, that Miss Eleanor,' mused Mrs Cruickshank, sipping her sloe cordial and leaning closer so Rachel might hear her above the festivities. 'Such a nice young lady, too.'

'Yes, indeed,' agreed Rachel vaguely, her eyes and mind distant as the kaleidoscope of dancers, music and merriment swirled before her.

'Now she's grown, there'll be no shortage of suitors,' pronounced Mrs Cruickshank, her plump cheeks flushed from the tithe barn's warmth and the potency of the sloe cordial. 'Why, I've already lost count of the young swains begging dances. You mark my words, she'll break a few hearts by and by!'

Although Rachel murmured some response, her troubled thoughts were with Ernest Cumstock, journeying through the night to his bereaved daughter and grandchildren. And much as it vexed her to admit it, she couldn't banish that altercation with Fred Leach either, nor his veiled threat. The man would seize upon any opportunity to close Ma's school! Without a teacher, how was Rachel to argue for keeping it open?

Engrossed in the turmoil surely lying ahead, she was unaware of a debonair gentleman purposefully approaching her.

'May I claim the next dance, Rachel?'

Startled, she raised her face sharply, and looked directly into a handsome face that had once been familiar . . . and so very dear to her.

'Hugh!'

5

'Jonas?' Rachel's voice was sharp. She was partway up the staircase, her arms filled with her youngest brother's freshly laundered and pressed white shirts together with a bundle of his neatly mended stockings. Hearing the heavy kitchen door open and shut, Rachel paused, looking down over the banister.

'Jonas — is that you?'

Quick, light footsteps across the kitchen's stone-flagged floor gave Rachel her answer even before Agnes Whitehead emerged into the passageway. 'It's only me,' she said, taken aback at her friend's harassed expression. 'Am I too early?'

'Not at all, Agnes,' replied Rachel at once. 'It is *I* who am running late! Jonas was in another of his foul tempers this morning and disappeared without doing any of his chores. I've attended to most, but he hasn't loaded the grain ready for us to take to the mill on our way to Brethwick. I swear, that boy becomes more sullen and belligerent by the day!'

'Given his recent promotion at Armstrong's,' commented Agnes, 'surely he ought to be in the best of spirits.'

'Jonas certainly worked hard to gain that promotion, but . . . perhaps it's gone to his head a little,' reflected Rachel. 'I can't fathom his ill humour and black moods, Agnes. He stays out till late, on occasion not coming home at all. I fear Jonas has fallen in with a fast crowd,' she confided bleakly. 'He's earning more money now, of course, and I'm certain he's started drinking and playing cards and dice in town.'

'Perhaps if your father spoke to him?'

'Oh, Pa scolds *me* about mithering Jonas,' revealed Rachel in exasperation. 'Pa says I should leave him be; that he'll come round in his own time. That's as may be, but while Jonas isn't pulling his weight at Pedlars Down, his responsibilities are falling upon Pa and

Edward's shoulders. It's neither fair nor practical.' She broke off, smiling ruefully. 'I'd best get on — these shirts and stockings won't put themselves away.'

After folding the garments neatly into the pine chest, Rachel tutted disapprovingly at the untidiness of Jonas's room. When would her brother learn to hang up his clothes? Rescuing the smart black coat Jonas wore to Armstrong's from where he'd tossed it across a chair back, Rachel found a clothes brush on the cluttered dresser and began giving the coat a thorough brushing. As she did so, a small, soft package slipped from one of its pockets. The folds of a clean linen handkerchief fell open, revealing a length of fine new ribbon the colour of buttercups. A gift for a sweetheart!

Rachel stared at the ribbon a long moment before stooping to retrieve it, carefully folding it once more into the handkerchief and replacing it into the coat pocket. Jonas had never breathed a word about a sweetheart. He must've met a girl in Liverpool, surmised Rachel, fetching her bonnet. Whoever could she be?

★ ★ ★

Starting downstairs and tying her bonnet strings as she went, Rachel was still musing over the buttercup ribbon when, passing the narrow window at the turn of the stairwell, she glanced down into the stable-yard and saw that the wagon was out and stacked with several grain sacks. Jonas must have returned and commenced his chores!

However, when Rachel and Agnes hurried outdoors, it wasn't Jonas who emerged from the store with another sack hoist upon his shoulder.

'Pa!' exclaimed Rachel, her lean features grimly set. 'What on earth are you doing?'

'What does it look like I'm doing?' Ben Warmsley got out a tad breathlessly, his weather-beaten face contorted with the strain of shoving the heavy sack up and over into the wagon. 'And before you start harpin' on, Rachel, I'm not so old and feeble I can't still shift a couple of sacks.'

'That isn't the point, Pa,' she argued, watching anxiously as her father pushed back his hat and rubbed the coarse sleeve of his shirt across his moist forehead. 'Loading this wagon was Jonas's responsibility! It isn't your job.'

'Enough, Rachel!' he cut in, stooping stiffly to retrieve his coat from where he'd slung it across the horse trough. 'It dun't matter whose job it is, so long as the job gets done. Your brother's grafting hard at Armstrong's and doing well for himself, so leave him be,' rebuked Ben curtly, turning away and heading for the tool shed. 'Wagon's ready.'

* * *

Stung and hurt by her father's abrupt reprimand, Rachel remained silent after she and Agnes drove away from the manor house. It was a fine, crisp day without a breath of wind, and the first falling leaves of autumn were scattering the winding lanes inland towards the mill. Presently, the grain mill came into their view and beyond it the flat, pale sheen of the mill pool, its surface so still it reflected the mill and clover-strewn sward as clearly as a looking-glass.

Two stocky grey Welsh Cobs were grazing on the sward, while the commodious covered wagon, which was becoming a quite familiar sight around Pedlars Down, stood at the far side of the mill house. Close by, painting the mill and its reflection in the mill pool, was Thadius Sawyer.

Hearing the rumble of the approaching wagon, he raised a hand in greeting. Setting aside his paint-box, he ambled across the sward toward them. 'Good morning.' He smiled up at both women, the broad brim of his hat casting shadows across his tanned face and clear blue eyes. Turning his attention toward Rachel,

Thadius's expression became serious. 'Beg pardon, ma'am, but have you any word from Mr Cumstock?'

'Edward and I received a letter from him after Robert's funeral,' replied Rachel. 'Ernest is remaining in Birmingham with Mary and the children. I'm packing up the rest of his belongings and sending them on.'

'If you write, will you please give Mr Cumstock my regards?' said Thadius, pausing slightly before asking, 'What's to become of your school, ma'am?'

'That decision rests entirely with the village elders,' answered Rachel simply. 'But I'm determined my mother's school *will* survive, Mr Sawyer. Pedlars Down sorely needs our school — whether the powers-that-be realise it or not!'

* * *

After leaving the grain for milling, Rachel and Agnes drove over to Brethwick and exchanged their books at the Ladies' Circulating Library. It was only later, when they were taking coffee and muffins at the adjoining genteel tea-room, that Agnes surveyed her friend wryly.

'Well?'

Rachel glanced up from her muffin, perplexed. 'Well what?'

'You are truly infuriating,' admonished Agnes, her pretty eyes sparkling. 'You must be aware I'm positively *burning* with curiosity! It's been weeks since Hugh returned from America, and you haven't yet told me a single detail!'

'There isn't much to say,' replied Rachel, stirring her coffee deliberately.

'Fiddlesticks!' cried her companion in sheer exasperation. 'Watching you and Hugh dancing on harvest night was like turning the clock back five years. You looked positively radiant in his arms — I've certainly never seen you as happy since before he went away.'

Rachel felt betraying colour stain her pale cheeks. 'The moment I saw Hugh that night, and was near him again, the old feelings came rushing back,' she admitted uneasily. 'I wasn't ready to feel those things, Agnes. I never expected to feel such intense emotion ever again.'

'Old flames rekindled,' murmured Agnes, holding her dainty coffee cup with both hands. 'You do still love Hugh, don't you?'

'Yes. Yes, I believe I do.' The older woman drew a measured breath. 'But nor can I forget how, without a word to me, he decided to sail for America and make a new life there. I missed him so much. Not even you know how desperately I longed for his letters. But gradually they arrived less and less frequently. Then they stopped. And my letters to him remained unanswered. It took me a very long time to get over that, Agnes. To become resigned to never hearing from Hugh again, to never seeing him again,' confided Rachel painfully. 'Now, suddenly, Hugh is back. Courting me. Everything as though he'd never been away. And yet . . . '

'Rachel, don't allow your fear of being hurt again, or your pride, to stand in the way,' warned Agnes gently, reaching across the table to squeeze her friend's hand. 'Hugh is home — and you have a second chance for happiness!'

★　★　★

'It's chilly this morning, miss,' said Ruth, sitting back on her heels before the fireplace and looking across the elegant room to Eleanor, seated at the writing desk beside the window. The two young women were of similar age, and Ruth always waited on Eleanor during the Burfords' frequent stays at the Rutherford Hotel. 'Are you sure you don't want this fire building up?'

'Hmm?' murmured Eleanor, eagerly rereading Lieutenant Giles Pearce's latest letter. They'd danced together five times during harvest night. Upon leaving the tithe barn seeking a breath of fresh air, they'd strolled in the moonlight, talking and talking and discovering so many shared interests and ideas. The next morning, Giles had written to her, sending the most beautiful flowers ... Since then, Eleanor and the lieutenant had struck up a lively and increasingly affectionate correspondence, and ...

'Miss, are you sure?' Ruth said again, a bit louder this time. 'You don't want this fire building up?'

'Oh, yes. Yes, quite sure,' replied Eleanor absently, raising thoughtful eyes from Giles's letter and her reply, which lay before her on the writing slope but had not yet progressed beyond her thanks and appreciation for his family's gracious invitation that she and her grandmother visit their home, Thornfield. 'I shall be out most of today.'

'Be sure to wrap up well then,' advised Ruth, gathering the scuttle, dust-pan and brushes. 'That wind's keen as a knife.'

Eleanor turned in the deeply-upholstered chair to face the maid. 'Ruth, do you have a sweetheart?'

'No, miss. I live in, y'see. The hotel don't let us have gentlemen friends,' she answered at once, but her mouth twitched mischievously. 'Mind, I do have a fancy for one of the boot-boys — but we'd both be out on our ears if the hotel finds out we're seeing each other on the sly. What about you, miss — have you got a beau?'

'Yes — or at least, I did have. Now I'm not so sure.' Her attention momentarily drifted to Lieutenant Pearce's letter. 'Jonas and I had a foolish squabble about my attending the harvest dance in our village, and we haven't seen each other since that afternoon. I've walked every day in Boyo's Wood, where we've met since childhood, but Jonas hasn't come.'

'Sounds like he's in a right sulk.'

'It's stubborn and childish of him to have stayed away, but I do miss him, Ruth. I worry about him, too. Jonas can be very hot-headed and reckless. He does things without any thought for the consequences.'

Ruth nodded sagely. 'Lads are like that.'

'I need to know where I stand,' declared Eleanor firmly. 'Whether Jonas and I are still sweethearts, or if all is over between us. And I intend finding out — today!'

'Why, miss,' gasped Ruth, wide-eyed, 'whatever are you going to do?'

Eleanor didn't reply at once; merely folded Lieutenant Giles Pearce's letter carefully and tucked it into her little embroidered purse. 'Confront him!'

★ ★ ★

Eleanor was familiar with the hours of business Jonas kept at the cotton merchant's, for whenever she and her grandmother were staying at the Rutherford, Eleanor and Jonas often contrived to meet at midday in the stationer's shop that stood across the street from Armstrong's.

A little before noon, Eleanor was browsing the well-stocked shelves and displays of pens, nibs, inks, wells, sand-casters, sealing wax, papers, bindings and sundry other writing materials, all the while watching for Jonas. The instant he appeared, she strode from the stationer's and crossed the street. At first sight of her, Jonas visibly faltered.

'What are *you* doing here?'

'Waiting for you,' she answered resolutely, continuing hotly, 'I haven't seen or heard from you for weeks! If you no longer wish to see me, Jonas, you might at least have the decency to tell me.'

'Don't want to see you?' he echoed in disbelief, raking a hand through his hair. 'I've done nowt but want to see you.'

'Why haven't you, then?' she challenged. 'I've walked in Boyo's Wood each morning as usual, been in the village as usual, at church, along the beach ... You've had plenty of opportunities to see me.'

'Aye,' he admitted, shamefaced. 'Aye, I have. That afternoon in the tithe barn — you were right, Lenny. It was *me* who was wrong — dead wrong. And I've kept putting off facing you about it. Telling you how sorry I am — for everything.'

'Jonas,' she sighed, 'you're hopeless!'

'I'm a fool.' He met her gaze steadily. 'I got riled up, and the last straw was seeing you with that lieutenant. Him whispering in your ear, putting his arms round you like he had a right — '

'You saw me?' Eleanor rounded on him. 'You were there, at the harvest dance — spying on me?'

'No! I mean aye, I were there right enough. But I wasn't spying on you! I wanted to see you, that's all,' Jonas blurted in despair. 'Can you not understand? You mean everything to me! I've never been so miserable my whole life as these past weeks,' he declared desperately. 'More than anything, Lenny, I want things like they

164

were between us. Can we go back to how we used to be?'

Eleanor nodded, her eyes shining. Impulsively, Jonas grasped both her hands and held them tightly. 'Will I see you later, at home?' he ventured eagerly. 'In Boyo's Wood?'

'We're staying at the Rutherford until the end of next week,' she answered. 'Grandma has business at Swann Burford and various charitable meetings.'

'Will you be — ' He broke off at the approaching hurly-burly, hastily drawing Eleanor into an alleyway and clear of the street.

Press gangers armed with cutlasses and cudgels were marching some three score forcibly recruited crewmen through the town toward the Liverpool Rendezvous, amidst shouts and jeers from onlookers and accompanied by an angry mob hurling stones and pelting the gangsmen with broken bottles.

'One of our ships, the *Endeavour*, sailed into port last night,' remarked

Eleanor, observing the commotion impassively. 'Grandma insisted upon going aboard before our crew came ashore to warn them the Hawks were abroad throughout the town, and further up along the coast, too. Losses in battle have recently been severe, and the navy sorely needs every man, experienced sailor or otherwise, it can muster,' she reasoned, considering the impressed recruits shambling by, many of whom had been rounded up from taverns and were still the worse for drink. 'So the Admiralty is relying more and more upon the Impress Service recruiting crews to man His Majesty's Ships.'

Jonas didn't reply. He paid scant attention to news of the war, and didn't share Eleanor's avid interest in the sea and ships. When the pressed men and their captors had gone by, he led Eleanor back onto the street and went on with what he'd started to ask.

'Can you get away one day next week?'

'I expect so. Why?'

'Brierley Fair's coming up. Have you ever been?'

Eleanor shook her head, her expressive eyes glowing with anticipation.

'Do you fancy us going — spending a whole day together at Brierley Fair?'

★ ★ ★

'Today's the day!' said Reverend Greenhalgh with a smile as he carried a large box into the schoolhouse, where Rachel was airing, dusting and making ready the classroom and accommodation. 'All being well, Mr Allen will arrive with the afternoon coach.'

'And very pleased we'll be to meet him!' responded Rachel wholeheartedly, scrubbing the tiny parlour's stone floor.

She hadn't had any say in the appointment of the new schoolmaster, of course. That had been the village elders' decision. Rachel had simply been thankful and immensely relieved to hear they'd agreed to engage another teacher and so preserve her mother's school.

Reverend Greenhalgh, who sat on the elders' council, had told her that despite Fred Leach and several others arguing fiercely that now Mr Cumstock was gone and the school had closed, it should remain closed, so saving the village an unnecessary expense, the vote had gone against them — albeit narrowly — and a new teacher duly sought.

'Ernest had been here since the day our school opened its doors,' reflected Rachel, glancing about the rooms now devoid of the elderly man's homely possessions. 'I wonder what Mr Allen will be like. Much younger, I expect.'

'He's a Yorkshireman too, of course — but we'll not hold that against him! The elders' decision was taken on his letter applying for the post, his characters, and his willingness to work for the meagre salary the village can offer,' recalled Reverend Greenhalgh, adding, 'Mr Allen's from one of those industrial schools over Leeds way, and it struck me, reading between the lines, that our man's had enough of being a small fish in a big pond and fancies being the big fish for a change. Ours may be a little country school, Rachel, but it's going to be *his* school,' concluded the vicar soberly. 'His to run as he sees fit.'

* * *

Thadius Sawyer liked Pedlars Down. It was indeed a quirk of Fate that after receiving a letter, together with a small financial legacy, from an English lawyer, Thadius had sailed thousands of miles from where he'd grown up on a fruit farm in Sweetbriar, Connecticut to discover a Lancashire village that somehow felt like home.

Sure enough, sketching and watercolours were his passion, but cabinet-making was his craft, and Thadius had gladly offered his skills to Reverend

Greenhalgh. He found it deeply satisfying to be working alone in the stillness of Pedlars Down's beautiful old church. While he was refurbishing the ornately carved steps of the pulpit, it came into his thoughts that his forebears had once worshipped at St. Cuthbert's — stood before this very altar and made their marriage pledge, brought their infants here for baptising, and brought loved ones to their rest here.

Daylight wouldn't last much longer, and Thadius started packing up his tools. He was carrying them to his wagon when the afternoon coach drew up outside Millers Inn. Only one passenger alighted.

'Hello!' Thadius greeted the tall, thin man with surprise. 'You must be the new schoolteacher, sir! Folk often say it's a small world, and so it is. Good to meet you again!'

'I *am* the newly appointed schoolmaster, yes,' responded Reginald Allen stiffly, waiting impatiently for his baggage to be handed down. 'However, we've never met before.'

'It was a short while ago,' exclaimed Thadius, trying to jog the man's memory. 'I was driving back from sketching the Roman fort when you rode by and asked the whereabouts of some farm or other — Leach's Farm, if I recall right; but I had no idea, being pretty much a stranger.'

'You are mistaken,' Allen cut in tersely. 'I *don't* ride, and this is the first occasion I've been in Lancashire.'

Thadius narrowed his eyes. He knew he was right, just as as he knew the other man was lying. 'My apologies, sir.' He shrugged. 'Good day to you.'

Thadius headed for the glebe, loaded his wagon and hitched up the Welsh Cobs. He *wasn't* mistaken about seeing Reginald Allen on the road from the Roman ruins. Why on earth would the new teacher lie about it, and insist he'd never before set foot in Lancashire?

* ★ ★ ★

They'd arranged to meet under the arcade opposite the Rutherford Hotel, on the flower-seller's corner. Jonas got to the arcade early and, standing there across from the luxurious Rutherford, raised his face and surveyed the rows of gleaming windows, wondering which were Lenny's rooms. She'd often told him the hotel was like a home-from-home for her and her grandmother. Especially since her birthday earlier that year, Lenny had been spending more and more time away from Pedlars Down — away from him; not just staying in town, either, but gadding about here, there and everywhere with the old granny. Soon, the pair of them were off for a whole week staying with family friends at Thornfield, wherever that was.

Jonas glowered, stuffing his hands into his pockets. He'd reckoned that being promoted at Armstrong's and having proper prospects would surely make a difference to him and Lenny. But it didn't. She had this whole other life without him . . .

He swore under his breath and took to pacing the corner, his gaze never shifting from the doors of the Rutherford. He felt like marching straight into the lobby and waiting for Lenny right there for the whole world to see! He didn't give a tinker's cuss if her grandmother found out about them. He *wanted* Harriet Burford to know! Jonas wanted *everybody* to know that he and Lenny were —

He caught sight of Eleanor emerging from the double doors. With his senses pounding, Jonas was off and sprinting through the traffic to meet her.

'You look grand!' he murmured thickly, aching to kiss her but mindful of the passersby surging around them. 'It's a cold day and the canal's a fair distance away,' he went on. 'We'll get a hackney.'

'I don't mind the cold!' exclaimed Eleanor. 'Let us walk.'

'All right, let's!' he agreed heartily; and, arm-in-arm like any other young couple in love, they quickened their step through the grey, chilly morning toward the canal and a barge that would take them inland to Brierley Fair.

★ ★ ★

Brierley Fair lasted for three days, and proceedings were well underway when Jonas and Eleanor alighted from the barge, joining streams of other folk coming across country from all directions and heading for the festivities. The fair sprawled far beyond the market square out into nearby lanes and fields. Everywhere was colour, crowds, noise and flurry, and Jonas was in high spirits. He had his girl on his arm and the whole day ahead before she must return to the Rutherford and attend a formal dinner with her grandmother.

'Working at Armstrong's has been the making of me, Lenny,' he was expounding while they weaved through the crowds, browsing the enticing stalls, barrows, and booths. 'I know the cotton trade inside out, and I'm really good at it. Sam Armstrong and I see eye to eye. He trusts me, and we work well together,' went on Jonas solemnly. 'He says I've a fine future and I'll make my fortune from cotton, just like he did. Happen one day I'll go over to our company in America.' He grinned at Eleanor, drawing her closer. 'How would you fancy living in a fine mansion in South Carolina, Lenny?'

'I wouldn't!' She shook her head, laughing. 'I love our village, and I love living there with my family. I never want to leave Pedlars Down. But what about you, Jonas? What do *you* want to do in the future? Really and truly, I mean?'

'Really and truly?' Jonas rubbed the palm of his hand across his chin, pretending to consider, then bent to slowly kiss her. 'To be with you, Lenny,' he murmured against her lips. 'That's what I want . . . To always be with you!'

* * *

There was plenty to see and do at Brierley Fair. They watched the tumblers, jugglers and dancers, and the seven players acting out tales of derring-do in a shadowed corner on the fringe of the market square. They listened to the balladeers and the wandering musicians, avoided the quacks peddling cure-alls and love potions, decided against crossing the fortune-teller's palm with silver, and explored the cornucopia of goods for sale or barter.

'These wooden toys are beautifully made,' observed Eleanor thoughtfully. 'I think I'll choose some for my nephews and niece — Christmastide isn't so far off, and I can hide the toys until then. Oh, and I must have another look at those quilts! I've never seen such intricate designs. Grandma would really like one, and I'll get one for Madge, too.'

'While you're doing that,' said Jonas,

'there's a — a harness I want to haggle over. I'll not be long. I'll meet you by the quilts.'

Leaving Eleanor's side, he weaved through the jostling crowds to a silversmith's booth he'd spotted earlier. Jonas also wished to buy a gift — and the instant he'd seen the slender silver band set with a single yellow Welsh stone, he'd known that was the very thing. The silversmith duly inscribed the inside of the ring with the entwined initials LB and JW.

With his purchase safely tucked into his breast pocket, Jonas sauntered back towards the quilts, whistling happily.

★ ★ ★

For Jonas, their day at Brierley Fair ended far too swiftly. Night had fallen long since. They'd alighted from the barge in Liverpool and taken a hackney to ensure Eleanor would reach the Rutherford in good time for her dinner engagement.

Seated beside her in the secluded intimacy of the cab, Jonas deliberated upon the little silver ring burning a hole in his pocket. Should he give it to her now, or save it till . . . The cab slowed down as it approached the hotel, and his moment had passed.

'Today was how it should always be,' Jonas declared suddenly, watching Eleanor adjusting her gloves and bonnet. 'You and me together.'

'Yes, we've had a wonderful day,' she agreed. But somehow Jonas felt Lenny wasn't really *there* with him anymore. Part of her was already inside the Rutherford, thinking about the grand evening that lay ahead.

Handing her down from the cab, he held on to her arm while the cabby unloaded the parcels and a boy from the hotel dashed forward to carry them inside. 'Will I see you tomorrow, Lenny? Will you be waiting in the stationer's?'

She shook her head. 'Grandma and I are helping to organise a musical evening to raise funds for the War Widows and Orphans. It's such an important cause. Mrs Armstrong is one of the ladies on the charitable committee.'

'When can I see you again?' he persisted.

'We're returning to Pedlars Down at the end of this week,' she replied, hurrying towards the Rutherford's regal entrance. 'I'll see you then.' She squeezed his hand and was gone. They'd parted without a kiss.

Jonas stood alone on the dark street, watching Eleanor ascend the marble steps. The commissionaire immediately stepped forward, drawing open the doors and greeting her deferentially. She inclined her head, responding graciously before sweeping within to the fine-and-fancy, well-heeled society where Jonas realised he had no place.

* * *

There was scarcely any wind that November morning, but the cold was keen and cutting. During the night, sleety hailstones had fallen, burying the hedgerows with thick icy crusts, heaping up against the gnarled trunks of bare trees and filling the crevices between the cobbles in the stable-yard.

It wasn't yet daylight, and although Rachel couldn't see much beyond the kitchen window, she'd been aware of the creak-creak of the barrow as young Paddy Dewhurst trundled back and forth from the stables to the midden. Paddy was a good lad, hard-working and conscientious. He came promptly each morning, never skived, got his jobs done and then went straight to school. He was a bright boy who could read and write fluently and figure accurately. Ernest Cumstock had once told her Paddy was eager to learn, and if he continued his schooling would have sound prospects.

Wrapping a hunk of cheese and a loaf into a square of muslin, Rachel slipped on her wooden pattens and clattered across the cobbles towards the stables.

Paddy looked up from piling fresh straw into the last-but-one stall. 'Morning, miss. The latch on Clover's stall is loose — I'll fix it before I go.'

'Thank you, Paddy,' she said, sighing inwardly. Yet another of Jonas's chores left undone! When it got light, she'd fetch the tools and fix the latch herself. 'But you'd best be on your way, or you'll be late for school.'

The boy bent to his work, raking the straw thoroughly. 'I don't mind missing school.'

'That isn't like you!' exclaimed Rachel in surprise. 'How are you doing there?'

'All right,' he answered without looking up. 'You don't come and see us anymore, miss.'

'I haven't been invited yet,' revealed Rachel candidly. She missed calling into the school, talking to the pupils about their studies and listening to their reading and compositions. She missed chatting to Ernest about the boys' progress, and his plans for the school's future.

'Which book is the class reading?' she asked cheerfully. Ernest always rounded off each school day by reading aloud a chapter from a novel suitable for boys. 'Is it another exciting adventure?'

'We don't have a book anymore,' mumbled Paddy glumly. 'It's not the same with the new teacher. He doesn't tell us stories like Mr Cumstock used to. He doesn't teach us about interesting things like Mr Cumstock did. It's just not the same!'

'I daresay Mr Allen has different ways, Paddy, and we're fortunate to have another teacher,' responded Rachel, going on after a moment, 'Your mother wasn't with you and your father in church yesterday. Is she keeping well?'

'She's been coughing and sneezing,' replied the boy with a frown. 'And she's shivering all the time.'

'I'll look in on her later, Paddy. Meanwhile, this is for you.' She offered him the muslin bundle of freshly baked bread and crumbly cheese. 'Eat some on your way to school, and save some for dinnertime.'

'Thanks, miss!' Paddy grinned, shoving the bundle into his homespun coat and darting away into the dark morning as another barrage of hailstones battered against the stables' slated roof. 'See you tomorrow!'

$$\star \quad \star \quad \star$$

Rachel strode briskly along the headland with its clumps of straggling firethorn, stunted gorse and scattering of squat cottages to call upon Maisie Dewhurst.

'Come and get yourself warm by the fire, Miss Rachel,' greeted Maisie, ushering her visitor indoors. 'I'm all on my own — Patrick took the boat out with the tide.'

'He mentioned you were poorly,' said Rachel, unpacking her basket. 'I've brought some soothing linctus; and if you make a brew from this mixture of herbs, spices and dried orange peel, it should help with the shivering — both remedies are my mother's recipe.'

'It's kind of you, Miss Rachel,' said Maisie with a smile. 'I'll be right as rain in no time taking these — my mam always swore by your mam's remedies.'

They were sitting before the small fire, sipping their tea. Rachel noticed the copy of *Robinson Crusoe* Ernest had given Paddy standing on the chimney shelf, and remarked upon it.

'That book's his pride and joy!' exclaimed Maisie. 'It's grand for me and his da to watch Paddy reading, for neither of us can make out more'n a word or two. Mr Cumstock lent Paddy loads more books to bring home. Often times, Paddy'd read 'em out to us — such tales of adventure and olden times and faraway places you never knew the like of! Course,' she added, pursing her lips, 'things is different now. What d'you make of this new teacher, Miss Rachel?'

'I haven't had anything to do with the school lately,' commented Rachel ruefully. 'How is Paddy getting along, Maisie?'

'Not good, to tell you true.' She shook her head. 'There's a fair few lads don't bother going to school now. That new man's a rum sort. Mr Allen scarce says a word to folk in the village, and the boys fear him summat bad. Paddy mitherin' us about leaving school, y'know? Wants to go on the fishing with his da.'

'I'd guessed all wasn't well.' Rachel frowned in concern. 'But I'd no idea Paddy was so deeply troubled.'

'The lad's not settled no more. I'm for letting him pack in school — but Patrick'll have none of it. He's dead set on our Paddy getting proper learning and making summat of himself,' concluded Maisie, topping up their tea cups. 'It's only fitting for a man to want the best for his son, isn't it?'

★　★　★

Presently, Rachel took her leave and started inland toward the village. Clearly, much was amiss with this new teacher's methods! And if fewer and fewer boys were attending, how long would it be before the village elders decided to close the school rather than waste money keeping it open?

Rachel wasn't about to stand by and simply allow this threat to gather pace. Something had to be done! She made directly for the parsonage with the purpose of discussing the problem with Reverend Greenhalgh.

The vicar had no sooner shown her into his study than the urgent tolling of the church bell interrupted them. With Reverend Greenhalgh at her heels, Rachel sped from the parsonage and through the garden gate into the churchyard.

The south door of St. Cuthbert's was wide open, swinging back and forth on its ancient hinges. The bell abruptly ceased; and as Rachel ran up the steps to go within, Paddy Dewhurst hurtled out.

'Come quick!' he cried wildly, his thin face blanched with cold and fear. 'Da's boat's washed up — but I've looked all over an' I can't find him. *I can't find my da!*'

* * *

'In the grocer's, you know the interminable while Mrs Standish takes weighing out dry goods, so there were a number of customers waiting in the shop,' related Agnes, swathed in a borrowed apron and helping Rachel prepare steamed puddings. 'I couldn't help overhearing. Folk were saying it's been four days since Patrick Dewhurst went missing. And what if the Dewhursts have fallen out, and Mr Dewhurst simply decided to up and leave?'

'Nonsense,' interrupted Rachel bluntly, buttering the huge stone pudding pots. 'Patrick Dewhurst would never desert his wife and son.'

'That's exactly what Harriet Burford said!' exclaimed Agnes. 'She and Miss

Eleanor Burford were in the grocer's and had overheard the conversation, too. Mrs Burford said that when she and her granddaughter heard the church bell, they'd hurried onto the shore, and it was patently obvious what had occurred — the press gang have seized Patrick Dewhurst!'

Rachel didn't respond at once. She looked again upon the picture she'd carried in her mind since she and young Paddy, together with many other villagers who'd answered the call of the tolling bell, had scrambled down the fisherman's path from the scrubby headland onto the deserted shore. The tide's roar was subdued. It was on the ebb, leaving in its wake rivulets of grey saltwater between hard ridges of wet sand. The Dewhursts' boat, still bearing the day's catch, was hauled up and beached above high water on the shingle beneath the headland. Splashes of fresh blood stained the hull. Boot and hoof prints pitted the coarse sand surrounding the small boat and for a

distance down the shore, before peter-
ing out amongst the soft sand of the
grassy dunes. Patrick Dewhurst was
nowhere in sight.

'I believe Mrs Burford is correct,'
Rachel replied thoughtfully, adding
more flour to the mixture she was
rubbing in. 'The press gang — ' A quiet
tapping at the kitchen door interrupted
her, and Rachel raised buttery, floury
hands from the bowl. 'Oh, no — who
can that be?'

'I'll answer it.' Smoothing her apron,
Agnes crossed the kitchen and drew
open the heavy door. 'Hugh! How
delightful to see you on such a grey,
wintry afternoon!' she trilled with a
beaming smile. 'Won't you come in?
We're putting up winter puddings.'

Removing his hat, Hugh stepped into
the kitchen and looked beyond Agnes
to Rachel, who was standing behind the
laden table with a smudge of flour on
her face and up to her elbows in an
enormous brown bowl. 'Ah, I've called
at an inopportune moment.'

'Not at all!' cried Agnes quickly, turning on her heel and catching Rachel's eye purposefully as she hurried past the table and disappeared into the pantry. 'I do believe I've forgotten the onions, Rachel — I'll fetch some . . . '

'I had hoped to find you alone,' said Hugh in a low voice, his gaze upon the partially closed pantry door. 'Can you not send Miss Whitehead to the village on some lengthy errand?'

'Certainly not,' replied Rachel, briskly wiping her hands. 'Agnes has already tactfully withdrawn into the pantry in search of onions we most certainly do not require for our rhubarb and ginger winter puddings.'

Hugh's handsome face was crestfallen. Moving around the table, he lightly caught Rachel's shoulders and bestowed a kiss upon her forehead. 'I'm extremely disappointed! I had intentions we'd spend the rest of the day together, then drive into Liverpool for dinner with my family at Riverslie House.'

The clatter of wheels and hoofs approaching at speed sent Rachel darting toward the door. In a couple of strides, Hugh moved ahead of her, glancing outside. 'Stay indoors. I'll attend to this,' he said curtly. 'It's a tinker's caravan — you mustn't allow their sort to trespass, Rachel.'

'They probably only wish to water their horses,' she said calmly, joining him in the doorway and exclaiming, 'Why, it's Mr Sawyer! Haven't you seen his wagon around the village? He isn't a trespasser, Hugh; he's an artist and cabinet-maker.'

'No honest, respectable man lives like a gypsy,' muttered Hugh scathingly.

Rachel wasn't listening. She was rushing down the steps into the cobbled stable-yard. Thadius leapt from the wagon and met her, his tanned face grave.

'It's your father, Miss Warmsley,' he said quietly, looking down into Rachel's alarmed, fearful eyes. 'He's been injured. I'll need a stretcher or some such to bring him home.'

6

'Where is he? What's happened?' demanded Rachel in a low voice. Breaking off, her hand pressed against her mouth, she swallowed hard. 'Hugh,' she called over her shoulder to where he stood, grim-faced and stock-still. 'Go for Dr Caxton. Hurry!'

With Agnes and Thadius Sawyer following, Rachel sped into the manor house, heart and mind and words racing. 'Agnes, go upstairs and fetch blankets, quilts, and a bolster to keep Pa warm and comfortable until we bring him home. Clean linen, too. We may need cloth for bandaging and wrappings. Get the medicine chest — you know where it is, don't you? I'll come and help presently,' she went on, turning to Thadius as she led the way through the kitchen and around a corner into a stone-flagged passageway.

'Mr Sawyer, you said Pa will need a stretcher? There's a sturdy oak board in the scullery — I'll show you . . . '

* * *

Jonas couldn't wait to see Lenny again! She and old Granny Burford had been away staying with the Pearces of Thornfield — folk Jonas didn't know, from a place he'd never heard of. She'd be back home at Withencroft by now, and they'd fixed to meet in Boyo's Wood this afternoon. He'd managed to get away from Armstrong's early — after squaring it with Sam Armstrong, mind you — and so absorbed was Jonas with his thoughts, he'd been quite content for Blaze to set his own pace during the miles from Liverpool.

When they veered off the high road and turned toward Pedlars Down, Jonas paid scant attention to the covered wagon rattling from the direction of the manor house and crossing his path directly ahead. If he even noticed

Rachel sitting up there beside the American, it didn't cross Jonas's mind to wonder about the reason she was with him, or why Thadius Sawyer was driving hell-for-leather along the rough drovers' track into the hill country.

Ever since Brierley Fair, Jonas had been agonising when, and how, to give Lenny the little silver ring. A ring wasn't like a length of fancy ribbon or a bunch of flowers — a ring was different. Giving Lenny a ring *meant* something. So would her accepting it — if she did . . .

The time had never seemed right, reasoned Jonas, oblivious to the covered wagon bearing his sister and Thadius Sawyer vanishing at speed amongst the stunted, scrubby trees. Whenever it *had* felt right and he'd been ready to give Lenny the ring, courage failed him, and he'd put it off for another time.

Well, that time had come! Jonas decided confidently. She'd been away visiting family friends, but now she was back and they were together again.

There'd be no better day than this to give Lenny the ring!

He was first to arrive at the lightning bole in Boyo's Wood. Recent north-easterly gales had stripped the last leaves from oak, beech and elm, rendering the old trees bare and the woodland eerily light. The ivy looked greener, the mosses more velvety and the prickly holly glossier, its abundant berries vivid and bright. Jonas noticed none of it. Seated on the fallen bole, he watched without seeing a lone squirrel foraging for acorns amongst the dry russet-brown bracken. Too agitated to sit still, he sprang to his feet and strode over to the swift-flowing brook where Blaze was drinking.

Taking the silver ring from his pocket, Jonas held it tightly and started pacing back and forth along the brook bank, going over and over in his mind exactly what he'd say when he gave it to — He froze, hearing the swish-swish of Lenny's skirts rustling through the drifts of dry, crunchy leaves. Thrusting the ring back into his pocket, Jonas spun around. And she was there, in his arms again.

'It's seems ages since you went away,' breathed Jonas, drinking in her closeness and loath to release her. 'I've missed you something fierce, Lenny. I'm glad you're back!'

'So am I,' she returned softly, touching her fingertips to his parted lips. 'It's fine visiting new places, but it's even better to come home again.'

'You look grand.' Gazing down at her, Jonas suddenly noticed the silky buttercup-yellow ribbon rosettes adorning Eleanor's nut-brown velvet bonnet. 'You're wearing the ribbon I gave you!'

'All my own needlework!' She laughed up at him, snuggling closer. 'It's such a beautiful colour, like a splash of golden sunshine on a grey day.'

'I bought it the day I got promoted,' recalled Jonas, his arms about her tiny waist. 'But after we quarrelled in the tithe barn, I carried that ribbon around for weeks, wondering if I'd ever get the chance to give it to you.'

'I'm very glad you did,' whispered Eleanor, her eyes huge.

'Lenny,' he blurted impulsively. 'Let's get wed!'

'We can't. We're too young,' she replied simply. 'You don't come of age for two years, and it's even longer for me. We'd need our families' consent — and they'd never agree to our being married!'

Jonas drew breath to argue, but recalling what Pa had said on the night of the harvest dance, he knew Eleanor was dead right. His father wouldn't allow it. And as for old Granny Burford . . .

'We can elope!' he exclaimed urgently, rushing on with his thoughts and senses racing. 'Other folk have done it! We'll go away, get wed and come back. There'll be nowt anybody can do about it then!'

Eleanor stared up at him in disbelief, slowly shaking her head. 'We can't elope, Jonas,' she responded quietly, still within the close embrace of his arms. 'I couldn't possibly hurt Grandma and my family by running away like that. I feel bad enough not having told them about you and me being sweethearts. Besides, I want to be married here, in Pedlars Down — at St. Cuthbert's, with my grandmother and all my family around me.'

Jonas's arms fell away from her, and he took a step back. 'I'd give up everything for you,' he countered bitterly. 'Why aren't you willing to do the same for me?'

'Jonas, we'll be together one day,' she said gently. 'We just need to wait a while.'

'I've had enough of waiting, Lenny!' he cut in passionately. 'I've got a good job, earning good money. I've proved myself at Armstrong's and I've got a good future ahead of me. We might not be rich like some of your fancy friends, but I can provide for you. We'd have a good life!'

'I know we would. It isn't anything to do with wealth,' Eleanor insisted rapidly, reaching out; but Jonas angrily turned from her. 'Where are you going?'

'What does it matter to you?' He strode to the brook, gathering up Blaze's reins.

Hurt and suddenly angry, Eleanor marched after him. 'Jonas! You're being silly! Whether we elope is as much my decision as yours.'

'Aye, so it is,' he retorted, starting away between the bare trees. 'And you turned me down!'

'I did not!'

'What else do you call it?' he demanded without a backward glance. Flinging himself into the saddle, he weaved through Boyo's Wood at a walk; but once up onto the open road, Jonas rode for Liverpool town like the devil himself was at his heels.

*   *   *

Darkness had fallen long ago, but the moon wasn't yet risen. Necessity was compelling Thadius Sawyer to drive very slowly and with the utmost caution. He had only the dull light cast by the wagon's lantern to guide them along the stony drovers' track snaking steeply down through the hills.

'How are you doing back there?' he called. 'Has your pa come round?'

'Not yet,' replied Rachel. Her father was lying still and pale on the oak board, swathed in blankets and quilts. 'He's stopped shivering, though, and the bleeding's stopped.'

She was kneeling beside him, trying to keep him warm and cushion his wounded head against the jolts and judders of the tortuous journey. If only they could get him home quickly, where Dr Caxton and help would be waiting . . . But Rachel understood fine well that Thadius had no choice but travel at snail's pace.

With a prayer of thanks, Rachel eventually glimpsed the lights of Pedlars Down glowing between the gnarled trees and bushy evergreens surrounding the old house, and the wagon's wheels presently clattered over the cobbles into the stable-yard. Its lantern had already been spotted from the manor house, and the kitchen door flung wide open. Agnes was running down the stone steps towards them, with portly Dr Caxton in her wake. Hugh Armstrong remained on the top step, his tall frame silhouetted in the doorway against the bright lamplight flooding from the kitchen.

'How is he?' Agnes asked anxiously, gazing up at Rachel as she scrambled from the wagon.

'Pa's alive — but . . . ' Rachel shook her head, unable to say more.

'Sir!' called Thadius, looking across the stable-yard to Hugh, still standing in the illuminated doorway. 'Will you come and give us a hand here?' Thadius went on, turning to Norman Caxton, 'Are you the doc? Squire Warmsley was conscious when I found him, but he passed out and hasn't come round since.'

'When Mr Armstrong called upon me, he merely said there'd been some sort of accident,' remarked Dr Caxton, peering through the gloom into the wagon. 'What exactly happened to Ben?'

'I'd been painting up at the crags. When I was on my way down, I heard somebody crying out and went to take a look,' replied Thadius, hefting one side of the board bearing the injured man while Hugh Armstrong took the opposite, easing it carefully from the wagon. 'I reckon Squire Warmsley'd been repairing a barn roof. It'd caved in, and he'd fallen through.'

'Darn fool.' Caxton shook his head, accompanying the younger men to the house. He and Ben had been friends more than forty years. 'At his age, he should know better than to go clambering about on roofs!'

* * *

'I've lit the fire and made up a bed in the little sitting-room,' Agnes told

Rachel while Thadius and Hugh were carrying Ben through the kitchen and along the stone-flagged passageway into the warm, comfortable room. 'I wasn't sure they'd be able to get the stretcher upstairs, you see. And I've gathered together everything I thought Dr Caxton will likely have need of,' she went on, frowning in alarm at her first clear sight of the seriously injured elderly man. 'I'll fetch water for washing and bathing his wounds — I've plenty boiled and cooling. I'm making you a hot drink straight away, Rachel,' she concluded softly, briefly catching hold of her friend's cold hand. 'You've had a dreadful shock. You look all in.'

'Thanks for getting everything ready,' murmured Rachel, waiting in the passageway while Thadius and Hugh came out from the little sitting-room, but looking beyond them to Norman Caxton examining his patient. 'You'll need my help, Doctor.'

Halting in the doorway, Hugh placed an arresting hand on her narrow shoulder. 'You shouldn't go in there, Rachel! Let Caxton take care of it. Your father won't be aware of your presence, anyway.'

'I'm not leaving Pa's side,' she responded firmly, her gaze never shifting from the little sitting-room.

Hugh drew in a sharp breath. 'As you wish. I don't believe there's anything more I can do here, Rachel.'

'No . . . no, you must return to Liverpool. You have dinner arrangements . . . ' she replied vaguely. 'Thank you for fetching Dr Caxton, Hugh.'

Accepting the bowl, pitcher of hot water and warmed towels Agnes had brought from the kitchen, Rachel entered the little sitting-room and noiselessly closed the door.

★ ★ ★

Hours later, when Dr Caxton had departed and Edward gone to sit at his father's bedside, Rachel wearily emerged from the little sitting-room and found Agnes alone in the kitchen. Only then did Rachel think of Thadius Sawyer and enquire after him.

'Mr Sawyer didn't leave for some considerable while,' related Agnes, brewing a pot of fresh tea. 'Lest there was anything more he could do to help.'

'I don't believe I even thanked him!' exclaimed Rachel in dismay, gratefully taking the tea and gazing up into the younger woman's eyes. 'Mr Sawyer likely saved Pa's life, Agnes! Goodness knows how long he'd lain there, hurt as badly as he is and unable to move. Shepherds Barn is such an isolated spot..' She broke off, biting her lip and living again that moment she and Thadius had picked their way over the rubble and broken timbers into the barn; seen her father lying still and bleeding on the hard earthen floor.

'Your father,' ventured Agnes tentatively, topping up Rachel's mug of tea. 'He — he *is* going to be all right, isn't he?'

'Dr Caxton says his leg and shoulder

should heal, given time. It's the wound to Pa's head he's most concerned about. Pa's breathing doesn't sound right, either,' she replied, her arms wrapped tight around her as she sat hunched at the big kitchen table. 'He hasn't woken up yet, Agnes. Dr Caxton said tonight will be critical. He told us to send for him at once if- if anything . . . '

'Dr Caxton is a fine physician,' put in her friend gently. 'Your father couldn't be in better hands.'

'This accident should never have happened! Pa's not a young man anymore, nor as strong as he used to be — and would have us believe him still to be,' blazed Rachel suddenly, her hazel eyes bright with unshed tears. 'More than a week ago, Jonas promised faithfully to repair the barn before the winter fodder is taken up. Pa must've known the job hadn't been done, and gone to Shepherds Barn himself. But mending that roof was Jonas's responsibility! Where is he, anyway? Jonas

should be in by now,' she mumbled
brokenly, head bowed and the emotions
of the day finally overwhelming her. 'He
should be here ... Jonas should *be*
here!'

*   *   *

After Agnes had gone home and
Edward retired to his bed, an uncom-
mon hush settled upon the manor
house. With Rupert padding along at
her side, Rachel took a bolster and
blanket into the little sitting-room and
settled into the winged chair. Rupert
curled up on the rug beside her, his
chin resting on his big paws and one ear
cocked for the sound of the kitchen
door creaking open and Jonas arriving
home.

Rachel sighed. This wouldn't be the
first time her young brother had stayed
out on the town. Reaching down, she
rested her hand upon Rupert's silky
head. 'Looks like it's just thee and me
tonight, old fellow ... '

In the shadow-filled little sitting-room, Rachel couldn't make out her father's face clearly; but hour after hour her ears strained, listening for his laboured, shallow breathing as she kept vigil — and waited for this endless night to pass.

★   ★   ★

Norman Caxton had been and gone, and at dinnertime Rachel was knitting in the little sitting-room when she heard the kitchen door opening and closing. 'That'll be Edward in from the fields, Pa,' she said softly, rising from his bedside and drawing the blankets more snugly about him. 'I'll not be a moment!'

She met Edward hurrying noiselessly along the passageway. 'How's Pa?' He broke off, for there was no mistaking the relief and thankfulness on his sister's drawn, weary face. 'Has he come round?'

'A few hours ago. He's very groggy,

but he's awake,' whispered Rachel joyfully. 'Dr Caxton warned me it'll be many months before Pa is up and about again, but he's come through the worst. He's going to be all right, Edward!'

While Edward went in to sit with their father, Rachel busied herself dishing up dinner. Looking into the little sitting-room, she beckoned her brother come for his meal.

'Pa's fallen asleep,' he murmured.

'Dr Caxton's prescribed medicine to help him sleep easy,' reassured Rachel, nonetheless going to the bedside to ensure all was well. 'He said the best remedy for pain and recovery is plenty of rest.'

So it was with an easy mind and lighter heart Edward settled to his dinner. 'I've a mystery for you,' he said with a smile when Rachel joined him at the table. 'I've just been up to Shepherds Barn to finish the job poor Pa started. I expected to find all manner of disarray after what had happened up there, but there were no scattered tools, no broken timbers and slates, and the roof appeared sound.'

Rachel stared in astonishment. 'Could Jonas have . . . ?'

'It crossed my mind, but definitely not,' chipped in Edward, enjoying telling the tale. 'Anyhow, I put my shoulder to the door — you know how stiff that thick little door is — shoved hard, and it opened so easily I practically fell inside! The hinges were newly oiled and adjusted. Tools and ladders were stacked neatly in a corner, and even in the barn's poor light I could plainly see the roof had been skilfully repaired, along with several beams.' He grinned across at his sister. 'Who do we know capable of such meticulous craftsmanship?'

'Mr Sawyer,' murmured Rachel, her eyes thoughtful and serious.

* * *

Thadius Sawyer was camping a mile or so beyond the village, with his wagon and Welsh Cobs sheltering beneath the trees at the deep bend of the river. He was heating a can of water over the fire, and at Edward's approach stood up and strode toward him.

'What news of your pa?'

'He's out of danger,' replied Edward, going on to thank the American for everything he'd done for Ben — and for his work at Shepherds Barn.

'Anybody would've done the same,' said Thadius with a shrug, offering a tin mug to Edward. 'Coffee?'

The two men sat companionably around the low fire, its darting flames glowing bright on the dull afternoon.

'How's Miss Warmsley getting along?' enquired Thadius quietly. 'She'll be kept busy nursing your pa, I guess?'

'Rachel sat up through the night at his bedside,' said Edward, nodding. He added with a wry smile, 'And now that Pa's awake, she's having to watch him like a hawk to make sure he swallows his medicine and follows the doctor's orders. Pa's not the easiest of patients!'

'While you're a man down, I could maybe help around the place,' suggested Thadius at length, adding apologetically, 'I don't mean to muscle in here. Most likely you and your brother already have everything — '

'Jonas doesn't do much at Pedlars Down,' interrupted Edward grimly, tossing aside the dregs of his coffee. 'He didn't come home again last night, so he doesn't even know Pa's been hurt. It's very generous of you,' he went on, meeting the other man's steady gaze. 'We would appreciate your help at Pedlars Down, Mr Sawyer. Many thanks.'

'It's Thadius — and you're welcome,' he responded with an easy grin. 'I grew up on my family's fruit farm, so I can turn my hand to most jobs on the land and likewise fixing things up.'

'Such as barn roofs and doors that won't open?' queried Edward, returning the grin.

'They're my specialty!'

'The restoration you did on the

pulpit at St. Cuthbert's was beautiful. While Rachel and I were admiring it, the vicar told us that members of your family were once parishioners here.'

'Way back, on my mother's side,' replied Thadius, packing up the coffee pot and tin mugs. 'That Ma's grandfather, Kenneth Pottinger, had left his home here in Lancashire and sailed for America was pretty much all we knew until quite recently. A firm of English attorneys wrote us that the last of Ma's Lancashire family — a Miss Cassandra Pottinger — had passed away some years ago and left instructions for them to seek out any surviving kin,' he related, extinguishing the fire and kicking over the traces. 'The attorneys finally tracked us down to Connecticut, and we found out I'd inherited her property. My folks didn't care for making the journey to England, but I wanted to come see where our family used to live,' Thadius went on, fetching the Welsh Cobs to the wagon. 'Although I've been doing a lot of sketches and watercolours to take home with me, I haven't actually been out to see Miss Pottinger's house yet. It's called Grey-wethers — do you know it?'

'It's a few miles north of here,' replied Edward, mounting up. There was still enough daylight left for them to make a start carting winter fodder up to Shepherds Barn. 'As far as I recall, that old house has always stood empty and closed up, but my sister may well remember it differently. When you next see her, you must ask Rachel about Greywethers.'

'I will.' Thadius smiled thoughtfully. 'Yes, I surely will.'

★   ★   ★

After dinner at Withencroft, Eleanor slipped away from the drawing-room, leaving her grandmother reading the newspaper and sister Madge playing the pianoforte, with husband Malcolm standing at her side singing a romantic air. Eleanor's nephews and nieces were long-since tucked up in their beds, and she tiptoed past the ajar doors of their rooms along the landing to her own room. Once within, she didn't light a lamp but went across to the large corner window, curling up there with her chin cupped in her hand.

With heavy heart, she stared out into the dark night. Lights from the house were shining across to the fir plantation where, so many times when they were children, Jonas had stood amongst the tall evergreens calling to her with their special owl-hoot signal. She'd rush to the window, overjoyed to see her best friend waving wildly, urging her to steal away from Withencroft and join him in some adventure . . .

A gentle tapping on the door roused Eleanor from her poignant reminiscence. 'May I come in?'

Eleanor nodded, and Harriet joined her granddaughter on the window seat. 'You're unhappy, my dear,' she murmured, smoothing the girl's unruly chestnut curls. 'Can you tell me what's making you so terribly sad?'

'Oh, Grandma!'

Harriet opened her arms and Eleanor gratefully took refuge in the comforting embrace. Pouring out the regrets and sorrows tormenting her troubled heart, she confided everything about herself and Jonas Warmsley: their childhood friendship, their becoming sweethearts and falling in love, their fierce argument — and their bitter parting . . .

'When I was young — about your age — I too had a beau,' Harriet said gently. 'Like you and Jonas, we'd known each other since we were children. He wanted to marry me, but — like you — I believed I must say no.'

Eleanor now stared wide-eyed at her grandmother. 'Didn't you love him?'

'Oh yes, I loved him. Very much.'

'Then why didn't you marry him? Were you too young, like Jonas and me?'

'We *were* very young; however, that wasn't the reason,' replied Harriet at length. 'My father didn't have a son to inherit our family's shipping line, so he brought in Sydney Burford as his business partner.'

'And that's the reason you married Sydney Burford!' exclaimed Eleanor, aghast. 'Even though you loved the other boy?'

'Sydney was my father's choice for me,' Harriet responded simply. 'He was an honourable man, and a fine husband and father. I tried to be a loyal, good wife who was worthy of his affection. Despite the great difference in our ages, Sydney and I had a harmonious marriage. My son and I lost him far too soon.'

'What about your sweetheart?' queried Eleanor. 'Did he forgive you for turning him down to marry somebody else?'

'No,' answered Harriet ruefully. 'No, I don't believe he did. And I've always wished . . . Ah, but that's quite enough of the past! We need to put on our thinking caps and find a way for you to make peace with Jonas,' encouraged

Harriet, putting her arm about the girl's shoulders and hugging her. 'Why not invite him to Withencroft? Or perhaps when you see Jonas at church on Sunday, suggest you and he — '

'It's too late,' Eleanor whispered, hot tears stinging her eyes. 'Jonas made it plain he doesn't want to see me again. Everything between us has ended!'

* * *

Agnes offered to watch over Ben so Rachel might go into the village and catch up with her errands.

'Jonas has never before stayed out two nights running,' Rachel was saying, buttoning her winter coat. 'And this morning when Hugh called to see me, he was complaining about Jonas and how badly he's letting down the firm. Apparently Mr Armstrong gave Jonas special permission to leave early two days ago, but he hasn't shown up for work since.' She frowned, bending to pat Rupert who, sensing a walk in the offing, was milling about her skirts. 'Jonas has *never* been negligent about Armstrong's, Agnes! He may be slipshod about everything else, but he has never been late, never missed a single day's work at Armstrong's. So where is he? What on earth is he doing?'

The whereabouts of her youngest brother were still taxing Rachel while, with Rupert ambling beside her, she went briskly about her errands in the village. They were coming from the parsonage when the dog's head suddenly shot up, and with a howl of sheer delight Rupert took off through the lane gate, hurtling around the corner and from Rachel's sight.

Jonas! It had to be . . . But when Rachel hurried around the corner, she stopped in her tracks. For it was not her brother, but Eleanor Burford stroking and praising the happy dog.

'Miss Warmsley! Good morning!' Caught unawares, the girl hastily straightened up. 'He — he's a fine dog, isn't he?'

'He is,' responded Rachel, equally taken aback.

Before she could utter another word, Eleanor darted away — and as she did so, Rachel noticed the buttercup-yellow ribbon rosettes trimming the girl's nut-brown velvet bonnet. She gasped, thoughts racing.

Could Eleanor Burford be Jonas's secret sweetheart?

★　★　★

For the first time in her life, Rachel set foot on Withencroft land. Hurrying up the sweeping drive to the reddish-pink sandstone house overlooking the sea, she sensed that despite the generations of hostility dividing their families, Harriet Burford would not have her turned away.

When a maid answered her ring at the bell-pull, Rachel asked if she might see Miss Eleanor Burford. She was duly shown into an elegant, warmly lit drawing-room and found not Eleanor, but Harriet Burford herself.

Rising from the armchair where she'd been reading, Harriet greeted her unexpected visitor cordially. 'Miss Warmsley, good afternoon! Eleanor is out on the beach with her nephews, but I expect them back directly. I'm about to have coffee. Won't you join me?'

'Erm, yes. Yes, thank you,' murmured Rachel distractedly, taking the offered seat. 'Mrs Burford, I do apologise for calling upon you in this way — '

'Rachel, whatever is it?' cut in Harriet urgently. Stricken by the gravity of the younger woman's expression, her own face had suddenly drained of colour. 'What's happened?'

'My brother Jonas,' Rachel said, swallowing hard. 'He hasn't been home for two nights; hasn't gone into Armstrong's where he — '

The drawing-room door burst open and two rosy-cheeked little boys, well-wrapped against the wintry weather, raced in to their great-grandmother with Eleanor at their heels. 'We've had a lovely — oh, sorry, Grandma!' she faltered, astonished at seeing Rachel sitting there in the drawing-room. 'I didn't realise you had company.'

'Miss Warmsley is here to see you, my dear,' responded Harriet softly, guiding the boisterous little boys towards the nursery maid appearing in the open doorway. 'She's concerned about Jonas.'

Still in her outdoor garments, and with mittened hands clasped tightly in her lap, Eleanor sank onto the sofa and listened to the information Rachel imparted with increasing alarm and fear.

'Have you seen him these past few days, Miss Burford?' finished Rachel anxiously. 'Do you know where he is?'

Feeling wretched, Eleanor shook her head. 'That afternoon, he'd left Armstrong's early and we met in Boyo's Wood. Jonas asked me to marry — to marry him,' she got out shakily, continuing after a long moment, 'We had the most awful argument, and he rode away.' She lowered her eyes, her hands knotting. 'Th-that's the last time I saw him!'

'Jonas didn't go home to the manor house,' prompted Harriet gently. 'Can you think of anywhere he might've gone? Of friends he would call upon?'

'I've never met any of Jonas's town friends,' gulped Eleanor, striving to pull herself together and think clearly. 'But I know they gather at the Saracen's Head. Jonas stables Blaze there too, every morning before he goes in to Armstrong's.'

'The Saracen's Head?' queried Rachel, adding warily, 'I believe I've heard tell of that place!'

'The Saracen's Head does possess a quite notorious reputation,' remarked Harriet bluntly. 'In spite of its outward appearance of respectability, it's nothing short of being a den of gambling, drunkenness and wild revelry. And as such, the tavern attracts gentlemen seeking excitement and diversion like bees to pollen. It also offers board and lodgings.' She glanced at Rachel. 'Might Jonas perhaps be staying there?'

'It seems likely, doesn't it? I certainly

hope so,' sighed Rachel, rising to leave. 'My family and I just want to know where he is, and if he's safe and well. Thank you both, very much, for your help. Edward will go to Liverpool straightaway and make enquiries at the tavern.'

'The Saracen's Head guards its nefarious activities and the privacy of its regular patrons extremely fiercely,' cautioned Harriet, accompanying her to the door. 'It can be dangerous in the town to ask too many questions, Miss Warmsley. Warn your brother to tread carefully.'

'I understand,' said Rachel with a nod. 'I'll be sure and tell Edward.'

'You will let us know, won't you?' implored Eleanor, 'if you have news of Jonas?'

'Immediately,' Rachel promised. 'And you'll do the same?'

'Of course we will,' reassured Harriet, adding as Rachel stepped out into the chilly dusk, 'I trust Squire Warmsley is keeping well?'

'I'm afraid Pa's suffered an accident,' replied Rachel, explaining that her father was now on the mend but would be laid up for several months.

At the time, she'd paid little attention to Harriet Burford's polite enquiry, assuming it mere courtesy. However, after she left Withencroft and was walking home, Rachel found herself reflecting upon Harriet's concern — and how very badly shaken she was at hearing of Ben's fall . . .

★ ★ ★

'This isn't your concern, Thadius,' said Edward, glancing sidelong at his companion. It was late; a clear, cloudless winter's night with the quarter-moon pouring silver-white light onto the long road to Liverpool. 'Much as I appreciate the offer, you don't have to come with me.'

'I know,' replied Thadius, raising his face and staring up at the ink-black, starless sky. 'But you've no idea where your brother is, and this tavern is where you're to start looking. It seems to me that from what your sister said about the Saracen's Head, it's the kind of place where if a man goes in asking awkward questions, he might need a friend watching his back.'

Edward couldn't argue with that. They rode on, speaking little. Entering the dark, smoky town, they weaved through a maze of narrow streets before finally fetching up close by the Saracen's Head. They reined in a short distance away, concealed within deep shadows cast by the imposing commercial and financial buildings, and for a while watched the comings and goings at the tavern and its adjoining livery stables.

'According to Eleanor Burford,' commented Edward at length, 'in addition to gambling and drinking at the Saracen's Head, Jonas stables his horse here every day before going in to work at Armstrong's.'

'Is that so?' Thadius cocked an

eyebrow. 'Y'know, Edward, after that long ride from Pedlars Down, I reckon our horses need a good rub-down and a bag of oats ... '

They sauntered into the large, dimly lit livery. A wizened ostler was occupied with an inebriated young gent who was collecting his horse, and this gave Thadius and Edward an opportunity to gain their bearings. Almost at once, Edward spotted Blaze in a stall down at the far end of the stables.

'That's Jonas's horse.'

Before he could say more, the wiry little ostler hurried over with humble apologies for keeping them waiting. Edward bid him a good evening, going on amiably, 'We're meeting my brother tonight, and I see his horse is already here. Would you happen to know if he's staying at the tavern?'

The ostler cleared his throat and spat. 'Which hoss might that be, sir?'

When Edward pointed out Blaze, the ostler stared up at him suspiciously. 'You be young Warmsley's kin? I've bin tending his hoss, waiting on somebody turning up to pay the bill and take yon hoss away.'

'What do you mean by that?' demanded Edward sharply, his heart suddenly thumping in his chest. 'Where's my brother?'

The ostler's eyes narrowed. 'Are you squaring his bill, sir?'

Impatiently, Edward paid the man. 'What do you know of Jonas? Where is he?'

The ostler shrugged, carefully counting the coins. 'Last I saw of Warmsley, he were larking about with some other young bucks — every man of them three sheets to the wind — and heading for Askies.'

'Askies?' echoed Edward, catching hold of his horse's reins and striding from the stables. 'What's that?'

'Grog-shop, on the dockside. But you're wasting your time going down there,' sniffed the ostler, pocketing his money. 'You'll not find your brother and his pals ashore — Askies crimps bagged 'em.'

'Crimps?' echoed Thadius sharply, glancing down from the saddle. 'If crimps are the same here in England as back home, I guess they're not like the press gang taking men for war service in your king's navy?'

'Crimps are a different kettle of fish, right enough!' cackled the ostler, raising his voice to be heard above the clatter of hoofs on cobblestones as the two men rode away. 'By now, young Warmsley'll be aboard a merchantman bound for the China Sea!'

7

'After choir practice last evening while Edward was walking me home — he's taken to doing so now, you know; now the evenings are so very dark,' added Agnes self-consciously, blushing slightly. 'He was telling me how he and Mr Sawyer rode into Liverpool in search of Jonas, only to discover he's been captured by crimps! The word is unfamiliar to me, but before I had opportunity to ask Edward further, we'd reached my garden gate and had to say goodnight,' went on Agnes as she and Rachel cleaned and dusted in the quietude of St. Cuthbert's. 'Does it mean Jonas has been sent away on a navy war-ship to where the fighting is?'

'No,' sighed Rachel heavily, sitting back on her heels with the polishing rag in both hands. 'Crimps have nothing to do with the King's navy, Agnes. Crimps kidnap men and sell them to work on merchant ships.'

'Jonas has been sold!' echoed Agnes in horror, staring at her friend. 'Like — like a slave? Surely that cannot happen? Not in England!'

'I could scarce believe it myself.' Rachel shook her head despairingly, bowing once more to her work. 'According to Mrs Burford, the practice is rife in Liverpool, and many other ports besides. Crimps prey on men — whether they be seafarers or no — in taverns and other low establishments, drugging the ale and spirits. When victims are insensible, they're rowed out to a trading vessel in need of crew before it sails, usually for the China Sea,' she went on, biting her lip and adding bitterly, 'My brother's been shanghaied, Agnes. It might be years before he sets foot on English soil again!'

Rachel did not add 'if ever' — but that possibility was stark in the minds of both women.

Night was fast falling before Rachel quit St. Cuthbert's. A dim light still showed from the schoolhouse, and she thought nothing of it. After the pupils went home, Ernest Cumstock had often spent hours longer in there tidying up, marking exercises and preparing lessons. However, as she passed nearby, Mr Allen unlatched the schoolhouse door and boys started filing out!

Rachel was taken aback. The school day should have ended more than an hour ago. Why on earth were the pupils leaving so late? She was accustomed to seeing them burst from the schoolhouse, talking and nudging one another, skylarking about before splitting up and going their separate ways; but tonight the boys appeared subdued and dejected — and Rachel was struck by how few pupils there were now.

Paddy Dewhurst was the last to emerge from the schoolhouse. With his father's disappearance, the family had lost its breadwinner; and Rachel was aware that while Mrs Dewhurst had found employment as washerwoman out at Fred Leach's farm, young Paddy worked before and after school in the stables at Millers Inn.

'Paddy!' she hailed as the boy sped from the schoolhouse. 'Why has school finished at this late hour?'

'We got kept in again, Miss Warmsley,' he replied hurriedly, loath to pause in his haste to reach Millers Inn. 'Mr Allen keeps us in all the time, even when we've done nothing wrong! I've got to go, miss, else I'll lose my job,' finished Paddy, racing away. 'As is, my wages'll get docked for being late!'

Another of the older pupils, Maurice Hewitt, overheard the exchange and sidled up alongside Rachel. 'My dad says he's had enough o' this,' said Maurice, who lived some miles away at the granaries. 'I've chores after school, so there's ructions when I get home late. My dad says much more of it and he'll send me to school no more.' The lad shrugged and sniffed, slouching off into the night. 'I'd be glad.'

Rachel watched him go, then looked back at the free school in consternation. When the village elders voted to appoint a new schoolmaster, and Reginald Allen had duly arrived in Pedlars Down, she'd been immensely relieved and determined to support him in every way possible. But the man couldn't be doing much worse if he were deliberately trying to drive away pupils and have the school closed down!

Light still burned within the schoolhouse. After another moment gathering her thoughts, Rachel deliberately strode across and rapped at the door. It was drawn open almost at once and Reginald Allen stared down at her, his thin features dour.

'May I speak with you, Mr Allen?' she enquired crisply, stepping over the threshold when it appeared the schoolmaster intended Rachel remain on the doorstone. 'I shan't occupy much of your time.'

She surveyed the cold, dimly lit classroom. The fire clearly had not been lit that day. Gone from the white-washed walls were the colourful maps, charts, drawings and tables Ernest had devised to help his pupils learn. With a sharp intake of breath, Rachel noticed an addition, and a thoroughly odious one at that. A thin cane, long and whippy, hung from a hook bored into the wall behind the schoolmaster's high desk.

'Despite the lateness of hour and darkness of season, I saw pupils being released from school only a short while ago,' she said. 'Mr Cumstock always ended school promptly because most boys have chores to do afterwards. And mindful several pupils live four and more miles away, as winter days grew shorter, he'd conclude lessons much earlier than usual to ensure every child reached home before dark.'

'That may have been my predecessor's method,' Allen remarked indifferently, his back toward her as he cleaned chalk from the slate-board with a duster. 'It is not mine.'

Rachel pursed her lips in growing annoyance. 'I believe keeping the pupils late has become a regular occurrence,' she persisted. 'May I enquire the reason?'

'The boys remain at their slates until the day's work is completed to my satisfaction,' replied the schoolmaster coldly, turning to face her. 'They are lazy, insolent, and must learn discipline and application — qualities clearly lacking in their education to date.'

Reginald Allen strode to the door, drawing it open and effectively bringing their interview to an end. 'I remind you, this is *my* school, Miss Warmsley — and I intend conducting it in the most efficient manner possible!'

★   ★   ★

Harriet carefully wrapped the novel she'd chosen during her and Eleanor's most recent trip into Liverpool. Their prime purpose had, of course, been galvanising Swann Burford's seafaring and trading connections in a bid to discover onto which merchant vessel Jonas and his friends had been shanghaied. The quest had so far proved fruitless.

Fastening her cape and double-tying her bonnet to secure it against the gusty sea wind, Harriet set off from Withencroft. Rather than starting inland toward Pedlars Down, however, she wandered beyond the tumbledown boathouse onto the shore. Eleanor was walking along the water's edge, with Jonas's dog close by her side. It had been kind of Rachel to ask Eleanor's help in caring for Rupert while Jonas was away, reflected Harriet. She'd explained that Rupert was pining terribly for Jonas, and since the old dog was clearly devoted to Eleanor, it would surely help him if —

Harriet broke off her thoughts, returning her granddaughter's vigorous wave as girl and dog dashed across the sand. It wasn't only Rupert who was benefitting from the daily companionship!

'I'm so glad Rachel lets me look after Rupert sometimes,' exclaimed Eleanor breathlessly, laughing and dodging as the dog shook a shower of sand and saltwater from his thick brown fur.

'I was thinking exactly the same thing.'

'You know, on the morning Jonas started at Armstrong's, we met in Boyo's Wood and he asked me to care for Rupert while he was at work because . . . because after Jonas himself, Rupert loves me best,' Eleanor faltered. She gave a quick little smile and indicated her grandmother's cape, bonnet and neatly wrapped book. 'You're off to Pedlars Down then?'

'Very nearly,' replied Harriet, patting Rupert's wet head. 'I haven't visited the manor house in more than forty years.'

'I'm certain you'll be made very welcome there, Grandma,' encouraged Eleanor. 'Rachel and Edward have wholeheartedly taken me into their home. The animosity between our families is quite forgotten.'

'Not before time, either,' commented Harriet, adding wryly, 'Although it isn't Rachel and Edward I'm concerned about.'

'Well, Squire Warmsley is still confined to his sick-room, so I haven't actually seen him yet,' admitted Eleanor. 'I enquire after his health, of course, and believe he is slowly recovering.'

'I asked Rachel if I might call upon her father, and she said he is well enough to receive visitors,' Harriet remarked with a small smile. 'Although I can't deny I'm more than a little apprehensive how I'll be received by him.'

'Jonas did tell me Squire Warmsley holds a fierce grudge against Burfords,' conceded Eleanor practically, going on optimistically, 'However, when all's said and done, Grandma, the bad blood between Warmsleys and Burfords began generations ago. Your family — the

Swanns — were close friends with the Warmsleys, weren't they? It was only after you married Sydney Burford that you became caught up in the feud. So the ill feeling between the families actually isn't anything to do with you personally,' finished the girl brightly. 'Is it?'

Harriet raised an eyebrow, falling into step with her granddaughter as they started up from the shore. 'It's rather more complicated than that, Eleanor,' she said ruefully. 'Remember my telling you when I was your age that I once had a beau who asked me to marry him . . . ?'

★   ★   ★

'Thank you for coming this afternoon, Harriet,' welcomed Rachel warmly, showing her guest indoors just as Thadius Sawyer was on his way out. 'Have you met Mr Sawyer?'

After the introductions were made and Thadius gone on his way, Rachel remarked how generous the American had been with his time, and how very hard he was working with Edward at Pedlars Down. 'These past weeks we'd have struggled to get the work done without Thadius's help,' she concluded.

'I've seen Mr Sawyer around the village, and admired his beautiful restoration work at the church of course,' responded Harriet, considering the younger woman thoughtfully. 'He seems a fine man, Rachel. A very kind one, with a true and good heart.'

'Yes, he is,' murmured Rachel, tapping on the little sitting-room's door and looking within while Harriet waited in the passageway. 'Pa, here's Mrs Burford to visit you!'

'I'm laid up here — tell her to go away!' retorted Ben Warmsley bluntly. 'I don't want to see her!'

'Pa!' gasped Rachel, horrified. She turned to Harriet. 'I do apologise, Harriet. I'm — '

'That's quite all right, Rachel,' the older woman put in with a reassuring smile. 'Please don't concern yourself. I'm sure you have far more important things to do.' With that, Harriet swept into the little sitting-room, barely noticing Rachel noiselessly closing the door and leaving her and Ben Warmsley alone.

Propped up on bolsters, his head still heavily bandaged, he glowered across the room at her. Harriet caught her breath, shocked at how thin, frail and very much older Ben looked. But she merely shook her head in a gesture of impatience and disapproval.

'I have foregone a genial outing with my granddaughter at the Brethwick Ladies' Circulating Library to wait upon you this afternoon, Squire Warmsley,' Harriet commented sternly, striding further into the room and settling herself into the winged arm-chair. 'The least you can do is behave civilly!' She placed the package on the counterpane beside him. 'I've brought you a novel.'

When Ben made no move toward the

package, Harriet unwrapped it and planted the book on his lap. 'It's about a gouty Welsh squire and his household travelling around the coast of England and Scotland,' she announced briskly. 'It's Smollett's final novel, and is said to be his funniest. It'll make you smile.'

'Pah!' exclaimed Ben scornfully. 'I don't have time to read fanciful stories.'

'What else are you going to do while you're ailing?' she countered, eyeing the box of dominoes on the table beside his bed. 'There's surely a limit to how many games of bonesticks even *you* can play in one day! You were an angry, obstinate young man,' she admonished calmly. 'Now you're a stubborn, curmudgeonly *old* man.'

'Your tongue's lost none of its vinegar and sharp edge, that's plain to see,' he retaliated, leafing carelessly through the book. 'Is there a purpose to this visit o' yourn? Or have you just come to torment me when I'm poorly and helpless?'

'Not least because of Jonas and

Eleanor, you and I are going to heal this ridiculous rift between our families once and for all,' pronounced Harriet firmly. 'Before I leave this afternoon, Ben, I intend clearing the air about the past — our shared past.'

'If tha' must, Hattie.' Glancing up from his book, Ben Warmsley considered his visitor warily. 'Happen I'd best shout Rachel to fetch us in some tea . . .'

*   ★   *

While accompanying Edward upon Pedlars Down business to Lancaster, Thadius had seized the opportunity and visited the attorney who had written notifying him of Cassandra Pottinger's bequest. From the moment of signing the papers and taking possession of the worn, heavy keys to Greywethers, Thadius had been itching to take a look at his family's old home. But life around Pedlars Down was pretty hectic, and today was the first chance for all three of them to drive out there together. It was really important to Thadius that Rachel and Edward accompany him when he visited Greywethers for the first time.

The derelict house was screened from sight by horse chestnut, oak, sycamore and clusters of pine, their fragrant dark boughs sparkling with winter's first hard frost. Once-ornate main gates hung askew on rusted hinges, so the friends continued along the curving lane, at length coming upon a tiny gate set deep into an overgrown bank swathed in brambles and ivy. Squeezing through, they followed a narrow overgrown path winding between dense trees and shrubbery. At length, it opened onto neglected flower gardens, and suddenly there it was — Greywethers!

Thadius stood and gazed. Bright early-morning sun glistered across frost-encrusted knee-high grasses, tares and tangled bracken to the square south-facing house. Even at this distance, Thadius could tell it was solid and stout. Built from bricks whose orangey-red colours were weathered and muted with passing time, its seven chimney pots rose sturdily from steep grey-slate roofs. Rows of large many-paned windows on each of three storeys ensured the interior would be airy and light.

Thadius guessed Greywethers to be several centuries younger than the manor house at Pedlars Down, but nonetheless must've stood here a hundred years or more. Maybe his mother's family, the Pottingers, had built it themselves. What would it have been like on the day Ma's grandfather, Kenneth Pottinger, had bidden farewell to his kinfolk before setting sail for America to find his fortune in the New World?

Thadius shook himself back to the present. Whatever the story — and he'd likely never know much about the house's history — his family had dwelled here at Greywethers for genera-tions. All the way down the years to the last of the English line; to Miss Cassandra Pottinger . . .

'I *have* been here before, Thadius!' Rachel's soft exclamation came from a little way across the garden. He turned to see her beneath the leafless, gnarled boughs of a mighty oak. She was kneeling in coarse frosty grass, her mittened hands unearthing a bulky object from amongst fallen leaves and undergrowth. 'When a while ago you asked if I knew the house and Miss Pottinger,' she went on with a smile, 'I *did* remember her — and Greywethers — but couldn't recall how.'

'What's come back to you?' He grinned, striding over to join her beneath the oaks. 'What have you found?'

'A swing!' laughed Rachel. 'I must've been four or five, and Ma brought me here. While she and Miss Pottinger were seated on the verandah talking, I played on this swing! I can't remember Miss Pottinger's face properly,' finished Rachel, frowning as she tried to recall.

'But I do remember how very kind she was to me while we were here. Then, when it was time for us to leave, Miss Pottinger gave me a storybook about magical wild horses to take home with me. It's a lovely book, Thadius, with lots of beautiful pictures. Miss Pottinger told me it'd been her book when she was a little girl!'

'Do you still have it?'

'Of course! I've always treasured it,' went on Rachel, accepting his offered hand as she rose from the frosty ground. 'Ma used to say that when I grew up and married, I could pass the book on to my little girl or boy.'

Thadius held her mittened hand a moment longer than necessary, looking down at her and glimpsing wistfulness in her eyes and voice. 'That's a fine idea,' he murmured warmly. 'And I'm sure one day you'll do exactly that!'

'Perhaps,' she responded, looking away and bending to dust the frost from her skirts.

'Despite years of neglect, there's a

fine orchard of old varieties and a substantial walled kitchen garden,' called Edward, emerging from around the rear of the house. 'The stables, coach-house and outbuildings are all a good size too, solid and stone-built.'

'Really?' Thadius remarked, pleased. 'That's swell, because I'll need some-place for my workshop.'

Rachel glanced at him in surprise. However, it was Edward who voiced the question on the tip of her tongue. 'You mean you aren't selling Greywethers and returning to America?'

'Absolutely not.' Thadius beamed, his eyes alight. 'For sure, the old place needs some fixing up, but I intend to make Greywethers my home.' Taking the heavy keys from his pocket, he waved an arm toward the well-worn stone steps leading up to the carved oak front door. 'Why don't we step inside and take a look around?'

* * *

'Greywethers has stood empty for many years, and fixing it up will certainly take time,' Thadius was saying when the three were walking to St. Cuthbert's on the first Sunday of Advent. 'But I'm a patient man, and I reckon Greywethers is worth working and waiting for.'

'It's certainly a beautiful old house,' endorsed Edward. 'Rachel and I will be happy to help. With three of us working together, it shouldn't be long before you're able to move in.'

'Oh, there's no rush,' responded Thadius easily. 'I'm happy enough in my wagon for the time being.'

'When the worst of the winter passes,' adjoined Rachel enthusiastically, 'we'll make ready the gardens for spring planting. All being well, come summer you'll be eating your own home-grown soft fruit and vegetables!'

'Oh, I like the sound of that!' laughed Thadius as they rounded the green and St. Cuthbert's came into view. The Burford carriages were in the lane, and he could see Harriet waiting to one side of the church's west door. She was accompanied by her whole family and Squire Warmsley, who was wearing his Sunday best and seated in the wheeled chair Mrs Burford had organised for him.

After exchanging warm greetings, the Warmsleys and Burfords entered St. Cuthbert's together. They'd no sooner settled in their pews than Edward rose hurriedly, his gaze fixed upon Agnes Whitehead emerging from the vestry carrying music for the morning's service. 'Excuse me,' he murmured, edging out from the pew. 'I — er — I need to lend Agnes a hand.'

Thadius grinned up at his friend and nodded. 'That music does look pretty heavy.'

Presently a hush descended upon the congregation, and the first clear notes of 'O Come, O Come Emmanuel' soared up into the ancient rafters of St. Cuthbert's. Sensing Rachel stir beside him, Thadius inclined toward her, feeling the softness of her smooth dark hair fleetingly brush his cheek.

'How strange that after generations of bitterness between the Warmsleys and the Burfords, our families are brought together by Eleanor and Jonas,' she whispered close to his ear. 'Wherever in the world he might be this Advent . . .'

* * *

Rachel took her letter for Mr Cumstock to Millers Inn with plenty of time to spare before the mail coach passed through the village early that evening. She and Ernest corresponded regularly, and, according to his letters, the elderly schoolmaster and his daughter and grandchildren were getting along as well as any recently bereaved family could hope to do.

'This wind and rain shows no sign of letting up,' remarked the landlord, stooping to peer through one of the inn's low windows as he accompanied her to the door. 'You've a long walk home ahead of you. Sure you won't take a hot drink before you go out again, Miss Warmsley?'

'No, thank you, I must get back,' she replied, drawing her cloak closer about her. 'And the sooner I set off, the sooner I'll get there.'

'True enough.' The landlord nodded amiably. 'Be sure and give Squire my regards for his recovery, won't you?'

Head bent and best foot forward, Rachel scurried through the village, skirting the rapidly deepening puddles and water-logged cart ruts barring her path. Borne by a cutting offshore wind, cold rain was driving directly into her face, and she didn't even see the boy standing outside the schoolhouse until she'd almost passed him by. It was little Walter Cruickshank, the baker's grandson.

'Whatever are you doing out here?' Rachel exclaimed. 'You must go inside at once!'

'I can't, miss,' he mumbled, staring at his scuffed boots. 'I had to stand up and read, but I kept g-getting the words wrong, so Mr Allen sent me out and said I was to stay here till home time.'

Anger and outrage rose within Rachel as she gazed down at the hatless, shivering child. Walter was nine, small for his age and little more than skin and bones. A long, serious illness had taken its toll.

'You need to get warm and dry,' she went on, clasping his cold hand. Although Walter lived several miles away, his grandparents' bakery was but a stone's throw across the green. 'And I know the very place!'

'I can't!' His eyes were wide and scared in his thin, wan face. 'Mr Allen told me I was to stay — '

'*I'll* speak to Mr Allen,' she put in quietly, her own face grave. 'You're not to fret, Walter.'

'But I'll get into more trouble.'

'No you won't,' Rachel reassured him firmly, shepherding the shuddering boy towards the warmth of his grandparents' bakery. 'You have my word upon that!'

* * *

Rachel realised only too keenly that it was not her place to even question the running of the school, much less challenge the master's authority there. Nonetheless, she couldn't simply stand by and do nothing. She waited until the boys were released from school — some three quarters of an hour late — before confronting Reginald Allen for the second time.

'Today you saw fit to punish Walter Cruickshank by having him stand out in the bitterly cold wind and rain,' she said without preamble. 'Surely a reprehensible and irresponsible punishment in any circumstances, but all the more so given Walter is far from hale and strong since his illness. And despite my previously explaining the necessity of school finishing promptly, pupils are *still* being kept in late,' continued Rachel tersely. 'Yet you are fully aware most of the boys have chores to do after school — or, like Paddy Dewhurst, a job to go to, while several others face a very long walk home in darkness, are you not?'

'Such matters are hardly my concern,' commented Allen, repairing to his desk and turning his attention to the papers there.

'Then they *should* be!' retorted Rachel, stepping forward so that she stood before the desk. 'You haven't made any effort to get to know the pupils, their families, their circumstances and troubles or, indeed, the ways of life in this village, have you? When we last spoke, you told me Ernest Cumstock's methods were not yours — more's the pity for that!' she railed angrily. 'I have no notion what passed muster in your previous post, Mr Allen, but your conduct in running this school, and most particularly your lack of concern for the welfare of pupils in your charge, will not do here in Pedlars Down. It will not do at all!'

'Are you, by any chance, seeking my resignation?' he enquired coldly. 'Then you have it — I resign forthwith! I was grossly misled as to the quality and nature of this school, and would never have accepted the appointment had I been aware of the true situation,' the schoolmaster continued, firmly escorting Rachel to the door. 'Those few pupils who do attend are ignorant, idle boys with no desire to learn. Frankly, it's an utter waste of my time trying to educate them. Pedlars Down school is closed, Miss Warmsley — and I very much doubt it will ever open its doors again!'

★   ★   ★

Eleanor was riding Blaze homewards along the deserted beach. The torrential rain and biting winds of recent days had finally abated, and a vast stillness settled upon the sandy shore. The tide was far out, leaving pools and skeins of clear, cold saltwater in its wake that sheared up in cascades beneath the roan's pounding hoofs.

She was giving Blaze his head, just as Jonas had shown her when they were still children and he was teaching Eleanor to ride. The horse was effortlessly, swiftly, covering the miles for the sheer joy and exhilaration of running free. When by and by Blaze slowed his pace, Eleanor leaned forward, stroking his neck. They were ambling now, not even disturbing clouds of herring gulls, oyster catchers and tawny grey dunlins foraging where the tide had been.

Eleanor was deep in thought. Since hearing that Reginald Allen had left the village, she'd been turning an idea over and over in her mind. It was an ambitious one — probably a very presumptuous one — and part of her was reluctant to even broach the subject.

Instead of veering up from the shore and taking Blaze straight home to Pedlars Down, she continued along the hard, damp sand towards Withencroft. She wanted her grandmother's opinion, and her guidance.

An hour later, Eleanor rode Blaze to the manor house. After removing his saddle, rubbing him down and settling the spirited roan into his stall, she went from the stables and crossed the cobbled yard.

'One in, one out,' said Edward with a grin, hailing her from the well. 'Rupert's indoors waiting for you.'

Despite her apprehension, Eleanor laughed. 'We're off for a nice dry walk in Boyo's Wood this afternoon. Actually, I was hoping to see Rachel, too,' she added soberly. 'Is she at home?'

Edward nodded. 'If she isn't in the kitchen, you'll find her sewing in the hall — Rachel's making a new dress for the Lord Mayor's banquet.'

'It sounds awfully grand.'

'Hugh Armstrong has asked Rachel to accompany him.'

Edward's forehead creased into a frown and, sensing his disapproval of the prosperous cotton merchant who was courting his sister, Eleanor said nothing more.

★ ★ ★

Bread was baking, cooking pots simmering, and a batch of pies cooling on the table when Eleanor entered the empty kitchen. She heard a great bark, the clicking of claws on stone flags, and Rupert hurtled in from the passageway to greet her. With the happy dog swaggering at her side, she went in search of Rachel — and found her in the great hall.

Although Eleanor was now a frequent visitor to the manor house, she hadn't set foot in the great hall since childhood. Drawing an unsteady breath, she looked around the cavernous oblong hall with its massive fireplace, gigantic Jacobean long-table and five-sided stained-glass compass window. The richly coloured panes were shedding vivid pools of blue, red, green and gold across the worn-smooth stone flags, exactly as they had upon that spring afternoon long, long ago . . . She'd only recently arrived in Pedlars Down then, but she and Jonas were fast becoming great pals! He'd smuggled her into the manor house and shown her a heavy gold coin wedged into the grain of an oak upright at the edge of the compass window. *Pirate's gold*, he'd told her —

'Hello, Eleanor!' said Rachel with a smile, glancing up from beading the bodice of her new dress. 'I didn't hear you come in.'

'May I have a word?' asked Eleanor hesitantly. 'Well, ask you something, really.'

'Of course,' responded Rachel, rising from one of the three-legged plumwood chairs in the compass window. 'Would you like tea?'

'No, thanks. It's about the school, you see,' said the younger woman eagerly, joining Rachel in the window alcove. 'Now that Mr Allen has gone, could I teach there? I realise I'm not a

261

proper teacher like Mr Cumstock, or even like Reginald Allen,' she rushed on. 'But thanks to Grandma, I've had a decent education, and I've been helping her teach my young nephews to read and write. Like my grandmother, I fervently believe Pedlars Down needs the free school,' finished Eleanor emphatically. 'And, like her, I also believe it's scandalous that girls aren't allowed to attend! I want the school to be for boys *and* girls, and I'll work terribly hard so one day that will happen!'

'With all my heart, Eleanor — thank you,' responded Rachel simply. 'I remember my mother saying those same words. Our school was Ma's life's work, and with you as its teacher it will be in safe hands.'

Eleanor's bonny face glowed, but then she gasped in dismay. 'What about the village elders?'

'We need to keep the school open, Eleanor, so I suggest you begin teaching immediately,' reasoned Rachel thoughtfully, adding, 'The school is not without friends on the elders' council. With help from the vicar, Dr Caxton and our other supporters, we'll try to win back those boys who've stopped attending while encouraging new pupils to enrol. Hopefully, by the time the elders' council meets to discuss Reginald Allen's hasty departure, we'll present a sound solution for the school's future.'

'Yes, that's exactly what we must do.' Eleanor nodded solemnly.

'Unfortunately, Reginald Allen quit with such haste and little courtesy, he did not have manners enough to return the school's key,' continued Rachel. 'I have a spare, as does the vicar, although he's loaned his to Thadius — who has offered to do much-needed repairs at the schoolhouse, particularly in the adjoining cottage. So you shall take mine.'

'I'll be at the school bright and early tomorrow morning,' Eleanor said when both women rose from their seats. 'I promise I'll work hard and won't ever let you down!'

'I know that,' responded Rachel warmly, tucking her arm through Eleanor's as the two turned from the compass window and started down the great hall with Rupert, impatient for his walk, bounding along excitedly at their sides. 'Come along, Miss Burford, schoolmistress of this parish — I'll fetch your key,' she went on, laughing as Eleanor threw one of her gloves for Rupert to chase. 'Then the pair of you can be away off to Boyo's Wood!'

* * *

'You look exquisitely, breathtakingly beautiful, Rachel,' declared Hugh Armstrong proudly on the evening of the Lord Mayor's banquet. 'I will most certainly be the envy of every man present.'

Rachel muttered an awkward thank-you. She never quite knew how to respond to Hugh's lavish compliments. They were descending the steps from the manor house's heavy oaken door to where one of the Armstrongs' carriages stood waiting. The liveried coachman drew open the door, and Hugh was handing Rachel inside when she spotted Maisie Dewhurst hovering in the darkness some little distance away.

'Something's happened!' exclaimed Rachel anxiously, stepping back from the carriage and looking up at Hugh, whose handsome face was now grimly set. 'I must find what brings Mrs Dewhurst here at night.'

'Whatever the matter may be, it will — and must — wait,' he interrupted firmly, his arm about her waist, bringing her back around to the carriage. 'If we don't set off directly — '

Rachel had already slipped from his grasp, hurrying across the cobbles towards Maisie Dewhurst. Casting an apologetic glance over her shoulder, she murmured, 'Please bear with me, Hugh — I have to see what's wrong.'

Maisie was standing stock-still, swathed

in a bulky shawl, her pale face appearing deathly white in the cold light of the rising moon. 'Miss Rachel, I'm ever so sorry to — '

'That's quite all right,' put in Rachel gently, ushering Maisie towards the kitchen door. 'Come along inside.'

'But you're going out! You're all done up,' she mumbled agitatedly, looking askance at Hugh. 'The gentleman's waiting.'

'That's all right,' reassured Rachel again as they went into the kitchen. 'Sit yourself down, Maisie. Is — is it news about Patrick?'

'Must be.' She pushed a crumpled letter into Rachel's hands. The wax seal was intact. 'It just came. I've never had a letter in my life. Patrick can't write, so it can't be him sending me a letter, can it?'

'Shall I open it?' enquired Rachel quietly, as the two sat side by side at the table. 'Do you want me to read it?'

Maisie nodded, biting her lip. 'Our Paddy could've read it to me, o' course, but I didn't tell him a letter's come. Didn't want him reading it in case . . . ' She gulped, rubbing the back of her hand across her eyes. 'In case it's . . . y'know.'

Rachel broke the seal and unfolded the paper. 'All is well, Maisie!' she exclaimed at once, swiftly scanning the neatly written lines. 'Patrick is safe and sound, and hopes you and Paddy are likewise.'

'Thank the Lord!' breathed Maisie, her mouth trembling. 'But where is he, Miss Rachel? What happened to him? When's he coming home?'

'Patrick has joined the navy and is serving aboard HMS *Gallant*. He's asked a shipmate to write to you on his behalf,' she related quickly, so Maisie might immediately gain the gist of her husband's situation. 'Patrick was taken by the press gang and held in the Liverpool Rendezvous for two days and one night before being ferried out to the *Gallant*. He decided to enlist and, once aboard, made his mark as a volunteer, not a pressed man. He says the *Gallant* isn't likely to see much action, so you're not to worry about him, and serving in the King's navy is a decent enough life for a man, except for him missing you and Paddy something chronic . . . '

Rachel paused while Maisie took in the momentous news, before reading aloud the letter word for word. 'There's an address for posting correspondence to Patrick,' she concluded, returning the precious letter. 'I'll be glad to write letters for you, Maisie — you have only to ask.'

Upon Maisie's hurrying home to show the letter to Paddy, whom she said she'd left poring over exercises Miss Burford had set the class, Rachel sped outdoors to offer her apologies to Hugh. 'You devote far too much time to the whims and worries of these people,' he opined furiously when they were finally in the carriage and travelling with all haste towards town. 'You never fail to place their interests before your own — and mine! You know full well being invited to the Lord Mayor's banquet is extremely important to me personally, as well as to Armstrong's. That we are setting off more than an hour late is because you're constantly at the beck and call of the villagers! Heaven knows I don't wish to disconcert you, Rachel,' he concluded, moderating his tone considerably. 'But I say this in your own best interests — you really must get your priorities to rights, my dear!'

★ ★ ★

Despite the inauspicious start to their evening, it was clear to Rachel that Hugh deemed the grand occasion an enormous success. She'd observed him exploiting several opportunities for enterprising discussion with the town's most important and influential men, so was hardly surprised to find him in high spirits during the return journey to Pedlars Down. When the carriage drew up alongside the great front door, a slight but keen breeze blowing in from the shore was sending drifts of grey cloud billowing across a starless cobalt sky; the ancient manor house was by turns bathed with chill moonlight and plunged into blackness and deepest shadow.

Rachel would have bidden Hugh good night and hurried directly indoors, but he stepped after her into the shelter and seclusion of the hallway, sweeping her into his arms and whispering against the scented softness of her neck, 'Is it so very wrong of me not to want to leave you?'

'I must go inside,' she persisted, moving deliberately from his embrace. 'It's very late, Hugh.'

As she turned away, he grasped her hand, pulling her close against him, lowering his face to hers. 'Rachel,' he mumbled urgently, his breathing ragged and his arms tightening fiercely about her. 'Rachel — marry me!'

8

She tensed within Hugh's arms. When a much younger woman, how oft — and how fervently — had Rachel yearned to hear Hugh speak those words! Pale moonlight spilling into the doorway was touching the contours of his face, and he had never before looked so handsome or desirable to her anguished eyes.

'Marry me, Rachel,' he urged again, stirred by her stillness and catching her fast against him. 'Become my wife!'

'I-I'm sorry,' she answered. Her heart was pounding, her throat dry, but Rachel raised her eyes to meet his demanding glare steadily. 'I'm so very sorry, Hugh.'

The quiet refusal was unexpected. For a split second he stared at her in sheer disbelief. Then pride and anger flared, and Rachel flinched beneath the scathing, relentless scrutiny.

'If I'd proposed before I left for America five years ago, you would have married me immediately, would you not?' Hugh challenged arrogantly, his cold eyes boring into her. 'Can I have changed so very much since then?'

'I don't believe you've changed at all,' Rachel replied, a hollow ache deep within her. 'Perhaps it is I who have changed.'

Without another word, Hugh bowed curtly and, turning on his heel, strode down to the waiting carriage. Rachel stood alone in the doorway, watching him leave, and was sorely torn. The carriage drove away at speed. Another ragged grey cloud drifted across the cold winter moon, plunging Pedlars Down into utter darkness.

Closing the heavy front door, Rachel stood with her shoulder blades pressed against its solid oak, her head bowed and eyes tightly shut. That she truly believed she'd made the right decision was scant consolation and no comfort whatsoever as she slowly started up the staircase to her room. She was no longer young. Hugh's proposal was her first, and — Rachel realised only too sharply — most likely her only chance of becoming a wife and having the children she longed for.

While unpinning her hair and stepping from her beautiful new gown, doubts crowded in, engulfing her agitated mind and tormented heart. In refusing Hugh's offer of marriage, Rachel had knowingly turned her back on everything she most wanted. Had she made the most dreadful mistake?

★   ★   ★

The Welsh Cobs' frenzied whinnying roused Thadius from sleep in the schoolhouse. Now that the worst of winter's weather was upon them, Rachel had suggested he bunk down in the unoccupied adjoining cottage and use the little stable at back of the schoolhouse to shelter his horses.

Tonight they were spooked.

Scrambling from his bedroll, Thadius dragged on his boots and ran to take a look around Meadow Well and settle the horses. It was a dark night with scant moon. Edged with arching trees and dense hedgerows, the verdant land followed the curving sweep of the river and wound away from the village. Thadius couldn't see or sense any prowlers. Everything seemed quiet enough — except for the Cobs. Sprinting the handful of yards across to the stable, he could hear their hoofs striking the timber stalls; recognised the shrill, panicked neighing. Then Thadius smelled the smoke. Not coming from back here at the stable — but borne on the still air from somewhere round front of the schoolhouse.

Racing back inside, he darted through the parlour to the narrow door connecting cottage with school — and froze. Sure enough, there was fire beyond that door — Thadius could hear it — but he'd caught the sound of something else besides. The scrape of boots on stone flags.

Moving swiftly and silently, he edged open the small door. Flames were rapidly seizing hold within the schoolhouse, illuminating the square room with leaping, brilliant flashes of fierce light. Beyond a heap of burning books, benches and boards, Thadius witnessed the arsonist.

Even as he charged in, the man turned from drenching the master's desk with pungent turpentine. Hurling the half-empty keg into the bonfire of books and timber, he wrenched open the schoolhouse door, fleeing into the night as the turps exploded into a raging wall of fire.

Choking for air, with both arms raised shielding his face and eyes from searing flames and spitting sparks, Thadius dived around the blaze and from the burning schoolhouse. The fire-maker had a head start, but Thadius was faster, stronger and younger. Tearing after him across

Meadow Well and plunging into the deep shadows of the riverside trees, Thadius finally brought down the arsonist as he was hauling himself into the saddle of a tethered horse. Breathing hard, his eyes stinging so he could scarcely see straight, Thadius held his captive fast, dragging him around and gaining a first glimpse of the man's face.

'For somebody who once told me he didn't ride, you sure were in a hurry to get onto this horse,' coughed Thadius as a shout of 'Fire!' went up in the village.

When the landlord of Millers Inn, the blacksmith and Walter Cruickshank came running in answer to his yell of 'Over here', Thadius was searching his prisoner for a knife or pistol — but instead discovered a heavy purse in the man's great-coat. Thadius whistled softly, pouring sovereigns into the palm of his hand. 'Well, well, look 'ee here . . . '

★   ★   ★

With Reginald Allen under arrest and bound for the county lock-up, the landlord of Millers Inn lit the hostelry's lamps, stirred the banked-up seawood fire into a passable blaze on the hearth, and flung open his doors to customers. For despite being the dead of night, it seemed the entire village was awake and out of bed, wrapped up against the bitter cold, and, now that the schoolhouse fire was extinguished and the culprit taken away, working up a rare thirst talking nineteen to the dozen about the night's excitement.

As an afterthought, the landlord sent one of his lads to carry the news to the manor house. Awakened by the lad's urgent thumping on the great front door, Rachel and Edward wasted no time in driving down into the village. A pall of acrid smoke hung on the still night air; the charred schoolhouse door stood wide open, and water that had doused the flames flooded out over the steps into oily pools. There wasn't a soul anywhere to be seen; it was clear those still abroad had repaired to the warmth and hospitality of Millers Inn.

'We must be certain nobody's been hurt putting out the fire,' murmured Rachel, alighting hurriedly from the cart. The lad had told her about folk making a chain, drawing water from both the schoolhouse pump and the village well, hefting along pails of water to hurl onto the flames. 'We must thank everybody for all they've done.'

'I'll see to it,' Edward responded quietly, taking in his sister's drawn, anxious face. 'You'll want to find Thadius.'

'Saw you coming!' boomed Norman Caxton, emerging from the inn. 'The situation's under control. Naught more can be done tonight.'

'Dr Caxton!' Picking up her skirts, Rachel ran across the green toward him. 'Is Thadius all right?'

'I wish my patients were half as hale,' reflected the physician heartily. 'He's somewhat singed, of course, but what can a man expect when he's run through a room aflame? You'll find your Mr Sawyer tending his horses,' he finished, considering Rachel with a knowing smile, 'should you wish to go looking.'

She was hurrying through the meadow gate toward the stable when Maisie Dewhurst caught up with her. 'I overheard summat a while back, but when all's said and done, Farmer Leach's affairs are nowt to do with me,' she blurted, chewing at her lower lip and glancing across to the smouldering schoolhouse. 'Then this happened — and it was Mr Allen who done it!'

'Whatever you have to tell me is obviously important,' responded Rachel, sudden suspicion flickering across her mind. 'Won't you come into the parsonage where we might speak privately?'

'I'll say my piece and get home,' Maisie answered decisively, her knuckles white as she wrung her hands. 'I don't want to get in no bother with Fred Leach, Miss Rachel — I need the job at his farm to pay me and Paddy's way until some brass comes from Patrick in the navy, but setting that fire was plain wickedness.

'I'd fallen behind in my work and stayed late to get finished,' related Maisie rapidly. 'It were past midnight before I were done. I was coming out the washhouse an' I heard Farmer Leach coming along behind the clipped yew. He had somebody with him and was in a right bad temper. I kept out of sight till they'd gone past. I didn't see the other man, but I heard his voice well enough — it were the schoolmaster, Miss Rachel!' She expelled a heavy breath, glad to get what she'd witnessed off her chest. 'Then Farmer Leach told Mr Allen to get the job finished and never show his face in Pedlars Down again!'

*   *   *

After giving his account of the night's events to the parish constable, Thadius returned to Rachel at the schoolhouse. 'Allen's made a full confession and put the whole story in writing, including Fred Leach's part as paymaster,' he related while they began the arduous, back-breaking task of raking and hauling still-smouldering heaps of burned, sodden wood and debris from the schoolhouse and piling it up onto a waiting cart. 'Their paths first crossed in Leeds, where Allen taught at a big industrial school. Leach knew he had ambitions to open his own school for the sons of wealthy families, but didn't have enough money to do it. After Mr Cumstock left Pedlars Down, the pair struck a deal,' went on Thadius, manoeuvring the blackened remnants of the schoolmaster's desk out to the cart. 'Leach would put up the capital for Allen's fancy new school — if Allen came to Pedlars Down and ran the free school into the ground.'

'Their plan very nearly succeeded,' admitted Rachel gravely. 'Reginald Allen drove away almost all the pupils and turned parents against the school. After he resigned, the elders would certainly have closed it down, had not Eleanor stepped in. She brought our school back to life, Thadius. Pupils who'd left began returning, and there's great hope for the future.'

'Allen reckons that was the last straw for Leach. Says he was in a rare fury and ordered Allen to destroy the school. Allen swears he was unwilling to set the fire, but . . . ' concluded the American scathingly, mindful of that heavy purse of sovereigns. ' . . . he did it anyhow.'

'Thank heavens your horses raised the alarm,' mumbled Rachel unsteadily, gazing around the sodden, soot-blackened room. 'What if the fire had spread into the cottage? The whole place could've burst into flames with you trapped inside! You might've been — '

'I wasn't,' he interrupted gently, clambering over a heap of burned debris and taking both Rachel's hands into his. 'Nobody got hurt. There isn't any damage that can't be fixed. And Reginald Allen and Fred Leach will answer for their crimes before judge and jury at the next assizes.'

★   ★   ★

'Allen's motive for doing what he did is plain enough: ambition and money,' Thadius was saying when they were taking a brief respite from their labours. He was brewing coffee on the Meadow Well riverbank, with the Welsh Cobs placidly grazing nearby on the coarse winter grass. 'What I can't square is why Leach was so dead set against the free school that he paid somebody to burn it down.'

'The school's always had some nay-sayers, but Leach has a particular axe to grind,' replied Rachel, washing her hands in a pail of clean water before opening a basket of bread, cheese and Lancashire brack. 'He's a loudmouth and bully, and has never missed a chance to stir up ill feeling toward the school. For him, closing it was the means to an end,' she finished bleakly. 'It's the land, you see. He's always wanted it.'

'Meadow Well?' queried Thadius, handing her a tin mug. 'How so?'

'The farm, quarry and Meadow Well have been owned by the Leach family for generations,' explained Rachel, sipping the hot, strong coffee. 'When my mother wanted to open a free school in Pedlars Down, John Leach — Fred's half-brother — and his wife donated Meadow Well. It included old outbuildings, the stable, and a disused workshop with adjoining cottage, which became the schoolhouse and master's accommodation. Mr and Mrs Leach had it repaired and fitted out with furniture, books, slates and so forth. They were a benevolent couple who did a great deal for this village, besides providing the school.'

'And Fred Leach opposed all this?'

'Oh, he wasn't here. There'd been a falling-out between the brothers many years before, and Fred had left Pedlars Down. It wasn't until John Leach died that Fred returned,' went on Rachel. 'Mr and Mrs Leach didn't have any children, so the family lands passed to Fred.'

'Except for Meadow Well.' Thadius nodded, getting the picture.

'Leach swore Meadow Well was rightfully his land, and he'd been cheated out of it,' she replied. 'He believes Meadow Well belongs to the Leaches, and his half-brother had no business giving it away.'

'So I guess Leach figured once the school was gone, he'd get Meadow Well back.'

Rachel's troubled gaze shifted to the fire-damaged schoolhouse. 'I recall Mr Cumstock once describing Fred Leach as an angry, ruthless man who'd stop at nothing to get what he wanted.'

'My, it's a right mess in there!' Paddy Dewhurst's exclamation came as he peered in at the schoolhouse door before running across Meadow Well towards Rachel and Thadius. 'Is it right we're starting lessons again tomorrow?'

'It is indeed, Paddy,' declared Rachel with a smile. 'Miss Burford has arranged with Reverend Greenhalgh for the school to meet in St. Cuthbert's for the time being. So be sure and tell the other boys it's school as usual — at St. Cuthbert's, until the schoolhouse is cleaned up and dried out.'

'I will, Miss Warmsley!' Paddy grinned, taking off across the meadow into the village. 'I'll go and tell 'em all now!'

The excited boy was gone in a flash; however, Rachel's attention dwelled in dismay upon the schoolhouse. 'Paddy's right — it *is* a right mess!'

'It sure is,' acknowledged Thadius, reading the distress and exhaustion in her eyes and hesitantly putting a comforting arm about her shoulders. 'It'll take time and work; but come spring, Eleanor and her pupils will be back in this old schoolhouse like last night never happened — you just wait and see!'

During those early months of the new year, winter tightened its grip upon Pedlars Down. For the Warmsleys and Burfords, the days were especially dark and bleak, for still they had no news of Jonas.

It was the longest winter Eleanor had ever known. She was kept busy teaching, of course, and soon she and her pupils would be returning to the schoolhouse, so there was much to be thankful for. Nonetheless, when the first flowers and sunshine of spring eventually appeared, the fresh, brighter days did little to lessen her remorse and grievous anxiety.

'Eleanor!' Edward called cheerily, slowing the cart on the track from the manor house. He and Agnes Whitehead were off out for the afternoon, and it was she who had spotted Eleanor wandering through the clover pasture with Rupert.

'Eleanor — over here!'

Absorbed in melancholy thought, only now did she hear and notice them waiting for her. At once waving a greeting, she hurried toward the track.

Edward and Agnes Whitehead had been friends for as long as Eleanor could remember, though it seemed to her their friendship was blossoming into something deeper and more intimate. She was delighted, for Edward and Agnes were two of the nicest folk Eleanor knew. However, upon approaching the cart and watching them together, she could not stifle the ache of loss within her, feeling her loneliness and longing for Jonas all the more keenly.

'We're making the most of this first sunny day of spring,' Agnes said with a smile, her pretty face touched with a becoming glow. 'We're taking a picnic to the Roman ruins — please join us, Eleanor! Rachel prepared our picnic basket,' she added, laughing. 'So you may be sure we're extremely well-provisioned!'

'Yes, do come along, Eleanor,' urged Edward warmly. 'Hop aboard — you and Rupert both!'

Eleanor shook her head but thanked them kindly, reaching up to scratch Billy's ears as the stocky black horse nuzzled into her shoulder. Lonely as she was, not for worlds would Eleanor intrude upon the happy couple's outing. 'I've lessons and exercises to prepare,' she went on truthfully. 'We have several new pupils, so I need to stay on my toes and not let the school down.'

'You're a splendid teacher, Eleanor!' exclaimed Agnes sincerely. 'Everybody says so. And when classes move from St. Cuthbert's back into the schoolhouse, there'll be room for even more pupils.'

'Girls too, one day!' Eleanor smiled, adding as an afterthought, 'Oh, is Squire Warmsley up and about? I was near the apple orchard earlier and thought I heard his voice.'

'Pa's not up, exactly — he's still using the wheeled chair your grandmother gave him. But now the weather's improving, he's certainly getting about,' Edward said with a grin. 'Poor Pa; it baulks him he's not yet able to do jobs himself, but the next best thing is barking orders to the journeyman and Thadius — who doubtless knows far more about growing fruit than the rest of us put together.'

The three friends conversed but a little while longer before Eleanor wished them a good day and waved the couple on their way. Turning into the shadow-dappled woodland, she followed a winding path. Emerging from beyond the oaks and holly bushes into warm spring sunlight, the brown and white timbers and leaded windows of Pedlars Down manor house lay before her. The swaths of wavering golden daffodils in Rachel's flower garden; the grey-fleeced ewes and lambs grazing on the thick, fresh grass; the whistles, calls and songs of birds . . . all evoked another spring afternoon long ago.

Suddenly, Eleanor's steps faltered. Recollections of Jonas were once again welling up uncontrollably, and with them the gnawing fears and sadness that never quite let her alone. She was haunted by the bitterness of her parting from him that dreadful day. The very last time she'd seen him. Would she ever have the chance to tell him how very much she loved him — had always loved him?

Given her upbringing within a seafaring family, Eleanor was only too aware of the perils, deprivations and harshness of shipboard life, coupled with cruel punishments meted out by unscrupulous masters and brutal mates to crimped men, especially landsmen who'd never before set foot aboard ship. Drawing in a painful breath, she started up toward the manor house with Rupert ambling beside her. Would Jonas ever come home again?

★ ★ ★

Thadius was making the most of the dry, brighter weather. The large doors of his workshop at Greywethers were flung wide; he'd spread sacking across the cobbles outside and was putting the finishing touches to a pinewood desk fashioned in the traditional New England style he knew and liked so well. It had been Rachel's idea that as a surprise for Eleanor he make a schoolmaster's — schoolmistress's — desk to replace the one destroyed in the fire. He straightened up and stepped back, critically surveying his work in the clear daylight. He never was completely satisfied with any piece he made, but was pretty pleased.

Turning at soft footfalls coming from around the side of Greywethers, he beamed as Rachel approached, dusting earth from her hands.

'That's the last of the kitchen garden planting — ' She broke off, seeing the pinewood desk. It had an inkwell, pen cup and pencil groove along the upper edge. The desk top was a writing slope that lifted to reveal a spacious compartment with four cubbyholes. Railed book galleries ran along both sides; and at the front, two panelled doors contained shelves and a large drawer. 'You've finished it — Eleanor will be delighted!' exclaimed Rachel, admiring the fine craftsmanship. 'You spend so much time helping Pa and Edward at Pedlars Down, I'm amazed there's any left over for your cabinet-making.'

Wandering past the desk and into Thadius's shadowy workshop, she spied eight ornate dining chairs ready to be carefully wrapped in clean sacking, packed in straw-filled chests and delivered to a customer in Rufford. Almost finished were a fancy card table and a sturdy wash-stand, and propped against the rear wall stood the beginnings of a large piece of furniture with clean, simple lines.

'What's this? Another new order?'

Thadius shook his head, joining her. 'It's a kitchen dresser, for the house.'

'For Greywethers?' she enquired, without looking at him. 'You really are making your home here then?'

'You're the reason I'm staying,' he replied softly. They were standing very close, but not touching. 'Will you marry me, Rachel?'

She gazed up at him sorrowfully, shaking her head, unable to speak. 'I-I'm needed at the manor house,' she whispered at length. 'Pa's on the mend, but he's still far from . . . and . . . and with Jonas — '

'Do you care for me?' Thadius gently interrupted, slowly lacing his fingers through hers.

'Of course I do!' cried Rachel passionately. 'Of course I do, Thadius!'

'That's all that matters,' he responded with a slow smile. 'I'm a patient man. I'll wait until the time's right. *Will* you marry me one day?'

Rachel nodded silently, and the love Thadius saw shining in her earnest eyes spoke louder than any words.

Slowly and tenderly, Thadius Sawyer drew Rachel Warmsley into his arms.

★ ★ ★

Rachel had an especially early start on the Sunday morning before classes returned to the schoolhouse. Thadius collected her from the manor house and they drove out to Greywethers, carefully loading Eleanor's desk into the wagon and taking it down to the schoolhouse. Set in place at the top of the airy classroom with its freshly sanded floor, whitewashed stone walls and shining small-paned windows, the pinewood desk looked very fine indeed.

By the time they went outdoors again, folk were beginning to congregate in the village for church. Maisie and young Paddy Dewhurst were talking with neighbours on the green, though when Maisie spotted Rachel and Thadius, she approached almost shyly.

'Beg pardon, Miss Rachel,' she said, 'but I've been looking out for you — I've had another letter from my Patrick!'

'You'll want to talk privately,' put in Thadius at once, moving away. 'I'll be over at the porch.'

'Oh, there's no need for that, Mr Sawyer!' exclaimed Maisie, adding proudly, 'Nor for you reading the letter to me, Miss Rachel — for I've read it myself! Our Paddy helped me with some words,' she went on. 'But I read most by myself. Miss Burford's been learning me. On the quiet, y'know. Just between the two of us. And I've started writin' now, so I'll be able to send my own letter to Patrick's ship!'

'What news is there from your husband, Mrs Dewhurst?' asked Thadius while they strolled toward St. Cuthbert's. 'Is he well?'

'He is that,' she laughed, ruefully shaking her head. 'Patrick's never happier than when he's on a boat. Mind, he makes light of the war and suchlike — tells us he never sees owt of the fighting. But I reckon that's so me and Paddy won't worrit as much about him.'

When they reached the west door, the Dewhursts went inside while Rachel and Thadius waited beside the porch for the Burfords and Squire Warmsley to arrive. Edward was already within, helping Agnes prepare music for the service.

The carriages drew up alongside St. Cuthbert's and the younger Burfords poured out from one, while Thadius stepped forward and handed Harriet down from the second. She thanked him, turning around to Squire Warmsley as he alighted awkwardly, leaning heavily on a polished hazel cane.

'May I take your arm, Ben?' murmured Harriet.

'I can manage fine well with this grand stick Thadius made me, thank 'ee very much,' he grumbled, but with a long-suffering sigh offered her his arm. 'Aye, go on then, if tha must. Remember this?' he asked while they walked slowly toward the west door.

'Our pirates' gold!' exclaimed Harriet at once, as Ben placed into her palm the misshapen Spanish coin that had been wedged into a beam of the manor house's compass window for as long as she could recall. 'When we were children, didn't we make up wonderfully daring, blood-curdling adventures about pieces of eight and treasure islands!'

'T'other day, I were thinking about that — and about your great-grandchildren,' he went on, folding Harriet's fingers closed around the old gold coin. 'I thought mebbe you could pass it on to the bairns, Hattie? Happen they'll fancy being pirates searching for buried treasure just like we did.'

She beamed mischievously. 'I'll make a skull-and-crossbones flag this very afternoon!' Arm in arm, they followed Rachel and Thadius into St. Cuthbert's and up the aisle. Harriet leaned closer to Ben and remarked, 'You do like Mr Sawyer, don't you?'

'That's a daft question. Course I like him! He's as honest as the day is long. Always first to lend a hand where it's needed,' returned Ben briskly. 'Aye, and a right good hard worker he is too.'

'Then why don't you say something?'

Ben eyed her suspiciously. 'What are you mithering on about now, Hattie?'

Nudging him, Harriet nodded towards the couple walking before them, heads close as they conversed quietly. 'If you'd let Rachel know she and Thadius have your blessing,' explained Harriet with a twinkle in her eye, 'there could be a wedding in this family before Christmas!'

* * *

Rachel and Thadius Sawyer married in late summer. Theirs was a quiet wedding, as they'd both wanted.

After giving the newlyweds her heartfelt wishes for every happiness and blessing, Eleanor called Rupert and slipped away to the solitude of Boyo's Wood. Amongst the joyous celebrations, her anguish at Jonas's absence was sharper than ever. He should have been here, with his sister and his family — with her! Eleanor needed to be alone now, with her thoughts and memories.

Weaving through the familiar woodland, alive with birdsong, fragrance and summer colour, she presently reached the heart of Boyo's Wood and sank down upon the fallen lightning bole. Since childhood, this had been their special meeting place. And here it was they'd parted so many, many months ago.

She was scarcely aware of Rupert rolling and growling contentedly in the tufty grass along the stream bank, until the dog suddenly leapt around onto all four paws and with a barrage of booming barks sped between the trees and out of sight. Startled, Eleanor sprang to her feet, spinning around as Rupert barged back through the bushes towards her — with Jonas in his wake. Eleanor cried his name, but no sound came.

Jonas ran to her, gathering her into his arms so tightly she could hardly breathe. 'I'm home, Lenny,' he mumbled, kissing her again and again. 'I never want to leave you ever again . . . '

Finally, he reluctantly released her and they sat together on the mossy bole. She leaned against him, eyes closed, listening to the rhythmic thump of his heartbeat until the brilliant heat of day gave way to mellow evening sunlight.

Jonas stirred, reaching into his ragged calico shirt and withdrawing a coarse string. He snapped it, and Eleanor caught a glint of something small and shiny falling into his rough, rope-scarred palm.

'I got this for you at Brierley Fair,' he said awkwardly, offering Eleanor the tiny silver ring set with a yellow Welsh stone he'd worn about his neck since the day they'd parted. 'But we'll go into town so you can choose the finest ring.'

Eleanor's fingertips upon Jonas's parted lips silenced him. 'This is the only ring I'll ever want . . . '

★ ★ ★

Eleanor had been shocked and horrified at how thin, haggard and very much older Jonas looked. During the following days and weeks, he did not say a word about his time at sea. Although Eleanor was desperate to ask questions and hear how he'd got back to Liverpool, she had heeded her grandmother's advice and not pressed him for explanations. 'He'll speak of his ordeal,' Harriet had said, 'if and when he's able to do so.'

Autumn became winter, and with Rupert gambolling ahead, the couple came from Withencroft onto the deserted beach. The tide was rolling in and they strolled along the water's edge, salt-spray and fresh wind whipping colour into their faces.

Unexpectedly, Jonas said, 'Half the crew on that merchantman was crimped. Most of us were landsmen, but a few old salts got crimped too. One was a jack-tar called McClusky. He'd been at sea since he was eight years old. He knew straight off we were aboard an unseaworthy vessel with an overloaded hold.'

Eleanor's blood ran cold. She kept her voice calm. 'What cargo was she carrying?'

'Coal, mostly. Bound for Shanghai. McClusky said we'd be lucky if she didn't go down and drown us all. We hit bad weather. It was all hands on deck, day after day, just trying to ride out the storm. Then McClusky told us we'd changed course and must be headed for the nearest port.

'We didn't make it. The wind changed. We got caught on a lee shore. The topmast and yards were being carried away. We could hear the ship breaking up . . . I was lucky, Lenny. I got to shore,' went on Jonas, his eyes distant as he stared out across the turbulent incoming tide. 'I stuck with McClusky. He got me a berth aboard a ship bound for England, and we worked our passage home. Soon as we docked in Liverpool, McClusky was on a packet to the Isle of Man.' He met

Eleanor's eyes. 'I headed straight here.'

Neither one said anything more. They simply walked together, watching Rupert splashing amongst the billowing, foamy shallows.

'Are you certain about not returning to Armstrong's?' Eleanor asked at length. Jonas had made the decision immediately he'd got home. 'You're not having second thoughts?'

He shook his head emphatically, grinning down at her and looking his old self again. 'Lenny, all I want is to stay in Pedlars Down, work with Pa and Edward — and court the village schoolmarm!'

* * *

On Christmas Eve afternoon, muffled against the bitter coldness and laden with bundles and packages, Rachel and Thadius left the bustle and merriment of the village and started homewards to Greywethers.

'A penny for your thoughts,' he invited.

'I was thinking about Christmas.' She smiled. 'And about your family preparing for Yuletide in Sweetbriar. They'll have received our parcel by now, won't they?'

She and Thadius had packed a chest with sketches and watercolours of Pedlars Down and Greywethers, stone jars of sweet preserves and tangy pickles and a huge Lancashire bunloaf, together with knitted and crocheted gifts for each of Thadius's parents and young sisters.

'I hope your family like the woollens,' Rachel added a shade apprehensively.

'They'll love them, and be glad of them,' responded Thadius cheerfully. 'Winters in Sweetbriar are long, snowy and very cold.'

Rachel had chosen a soft, thick wool for the scarves and mittens, spun on the ancient spinning wheel in the compass window at the manor house. The wheel had been passed down through generations of Warmsley women, and Squire Warmsley had urged Rachel to take it with her to Greywethers. She'd been touched, but refused. That old spinning wheel was part of the manor house. It somehow belonged to all the Warmsley women who'd gone before, and to those yet to come.

On the morning of her wedding, Rachel dressed and paused wistfully before the looking-glass. She was wishing Ma were here, sharing this happiest of days, when Pa tapped lightly upon her door. 'I fetched this from the store-room,' Ben said awkwardly. 'It's been gathering dust for many a year, so I've polished it up a bit. It still works fine well.'

'Ma's own spinning wheel!' gasped Rachel in wonder. She'd seen it before, of course, when she'd been a little girl. Ma had shown it to her, telling the story of how she'd brought the wheel with her from Cumbria when she'd come to Pedlars Down as a bride.

'After we wed, your ma always used the Warmsley wheel, so this one was put away for safekeeping. It's fitting you take her old spinning wheel with you to your new home,' went on Ben gruffly, reaching out and patting his only daughter's shoulder vigorously. 'It's what your ma would want if she were still here with us. You look gradely, lass,' he added proudly, turning hurriedly from the room. 'Right gradely!'

Thadius had set the spinning wheel before one of the large windows at Greywethers, and Rachel had already done some spinning on it — an especially fine yarn for the delicate garments she'd be knitting and crocheting during the months ahead.

Rachel drew a contented breath as the chimneys of Greywethers came into view, silhouetted against the low, yellowish-grey December sky. There was not a breath of wind, but the cold was cutting. Drawing nearer Thadius, she rested her head against his shoulder.

'Another penny — no, a silver shilling — for your thoughts.' He laughed, gazing down at her shining eyes and the gentle smile playing upon her lips.

'What are you thinking about?'

'Oh, just thoughts — very happy ones!' she declared, nestling closer still. 'I was thinking about families — about our families: Jonas and Eleanor, the Burfords and the Warmsleys, all coming together for Christmas at the manor house. If only your parents and sisters were here, too.'

'Once winter's over,' he said with a smile, 'I'm sure they'll come visit us.'

'I hope so. But just the same, I do wish your family could be with us tomorrow for the Christmas festivities at the manor house.'

'It's going to be quite a day,' he agreed quietly, kissing her. 'But you know what I'm especially looking forward to, Rachel? You and I spending a quiet Christmas Eve together at Greywethers — just we two.'

'We'd better make the most of being just we two, Thadius.' She beamed as they started up the curving stone steps to their front door. 'For by this time next year . . . '

Their eyes met in joyful understanding, and the first snowflakes of winter drifted down around the gabled roofs of Greywethers.

We do hope that you have enjoyed reading this large print book.

Did you know that all of our titles are available for purchase?

We publish a wide range of high quality large print books including:
Romances, Mysteries, Classics
General Fiction
Non Fiction and Westerns

Special interest titles available in large print are:
The Little Oxford Dictionary
Music Book, Song Book
Hymn Book, Service Book

Also available from us courtesy of Oxford University Press:
Young Readers' Dictionary
(large print edition)
Young Readers' Thesaurus
(large print edition)

For further information or a free brochure, please contact us at:
Ulverscroft Large Print Books Ltd.,
The Green, Bradgate Road, Anstey,
Leicester, LE7 7FU, England.
Tel: (00 44) **0116 236 4325**
Fax: (00 44) **0116 234 0205**

Other titles in the
Linford Romance Library:

THE MOST WONDERFUL TIME OF THE YEAR

Wendy Kremer

After ditching her cheating boyfriend, Sara escapes to a small village for Christmas, expecting to find rest and relaxation without the usual seasonal stresses. But her landlady, Emma, soon involves her in the village's holiday preparations, and the magic of Christmas begins to weave its spell. While Sara settles in and makes new friends, she also relishes the special attentions of Emma's handsome neighbour, Alex, and his young daughter. Could she actually have a future here — and is this Christmas destined to be her best ever?

OFF LIMITS LOVER

Judy Jarvie

Practice nurse Anya Fraser's adopted son is the centre of her busy life. But once her village clinic's handsome new senior partner Dr. Max Calder arrives, he is suddenly in her thoughts more than she's ready to admit. When extreme sports fan Max volunteers to help her with a terrifying charity parachute jump, they grow close. But Anya soon learns that the leap of faith she must take will impact on the home life she's fought so hard to secure.

HUNGRY FOR LOVE

Margaret Mounsdon

When celebrity chef Charlie Irons is let go from his daytime cookery slot, Louise Drew becomes his replacement. But with minimal cookery experience, appalling on-air nerves and disastrous culinary experiments, she is unable to sustain viewing figures and is sacked. She applies for a new job as a personal assistant with catering experience, but realises to her horror that it would mean working for Charlie Irons — and looking after two headstrong young girls. Is Louise up to the task, especially when Charlie's glamorous ex-wife arrives on the scene?

THE MISTRESS OF ROSEHAVEN

Rosemary Sansum

Left widowed and in debt, Rosemary Shaw has no choice but to accept an invitation from an uncle she has never met to come and live at his Rhode Island mansion, Rosehaven. But from the minute she arrives with her young children, she finds the place ominous and unsettling. Even as she begins to fall in love with the mysterious Will Hennessy, it seems that someone is prepared to go to any lengths to prevent Rosemary from becoming the new mistress of Rosehaven . . .